FURY OF PERSUASION

COREENE CALLAHAN

OLIVER
HEBER
BOOKS

1

Vyroth would've killed for a little quiet. A strange thing to wish for after spending two months alone. Days ticked by with no one to talk to and nothing to occupy his mind. Sixty days in what amounted to a hole. Solitary confinement with nasty undertones, given he was locked deep underground, location unknown, surrounded by the most powerful energy shield he'd ever encountered.

Miles of solid rock wrapped in impenetrable magic.

A supermax prison designed by a psychopath.

The mother of all mind-fucks for a Dragonkind warrior accustomed to fresh air and wide-open skies.

If heavy duty magic was all he needed to fight, he could've coped. Handled the mistreatment. Dealt with the soul-withering hunger. Remained patient long enough to find a way around the security measures. Lying prone on the uneven floor in his cell, Vyroth ran down the list inside his head. Again. For the umpteenth time.

Multiple layers of high-end security.

The best system money could buy.

Not easy to circumvent in his weakened state. But

with nothing to do but keep his mind busy, his imagination ran wild.

Everything was on the table.

Digging through the floor. Tunneling through a wall. Risking life and limb testing the energy shield for weak spots. He'd dreamed up all kinds of scenarios. Unraveled each one like a candy wrapper, with meticulous care, paying close attention to foot patrols and changes in guards, collecting the details, hunting for scraps of information to facilitate an escape.

Too bad none of it mattered.

All the careful planning amounted to less than nothing when he couldn't get past the first hurdle—the saltwater frothing around his little patch of heaven. Set in the middle of a raging river, the tiny island was diabolical. Brutal. Brilliant. A real fuck-you to his dragon half, given the salt water would kill him if he attempted to swim it.

He had to give the bastard credit.

Montgomery knew what he was doing. Had done his due diligence, discovered his weakness, then used it to maximum effect, giving him nowhere to go and even fewer places to hide.

Flat on his back in the center of the island, Vyroth opened his eyes. Same old, same old. Hard rock beneath him. The vaulted curves of the cave above him. Dragon-made, claw marks scored across the granite. He knew each gouge by heart. Had counted every fleck of sparkling quartz in the damp, stone cage imprisoning him. Lived with the maddening hum of the energy shield. Listened to the rage-inducing rumble of a river that never shut up.

Gritting his teeth, he stacked his hands behind his head and stared at the white vein bisecting the black granite above him. A pale slash in a sea of dark stone.

Something to look at while he descended deeper into energy-greed, his hunger so profound Vyroth didn't know if he'd survive it. He was close. So very close to tumbling off the edge into insanity. From slipping away and...

"Hellfire," he growled, fisting his hands in his hair.

He pulled on the strands. Pain streaked across his scalp as he fought to find level, but... no way around it. Desperation had come calling. He needed a female. Needed to feed before his dragon half shriveled up and died. Needed to get the hell out of Montgomery's prison and figure out what the hell was going on. Why he'd been ambushed, drugged, flown goddess-only-knew-where, and locked down.

Could be any number of reasons.

Could be any number of males.

He wasn't the most likable fellow. Social interaction wasn't his strong suit. He preferred when his fists talked for him, but that couldn't be it. He hadn't pissed anyone off of late. He'd been careful. Flown under the radar. No scuffles. No rough words exchanged. Zero footprint in Prague, a city he knew well.

His mission required stealth.

The quiet gathering of intel, the skilled tapping of information through informants friendly to his pack.

He'd been a whisper away from the truth—from uncovering new leads and following the trail. Intel remained scarce. Most reports were sketchy, but he knew enough now.

Forge was alive.

His cousin was out there... somewhere.

All he needed to do was find him.

Right now, though, Forge was on his own. Priorities must be established. Number one on his ever-lengthening list involved a long, thorough feeding.

He'd settled for a visit from a low energy female. Or better yet, a wee taste of one from home.

Brain burning, his mind circled the drain. Memories tortured him with thoughts of Aberdeen. Goddess, he missed his brothers. Missed Scotland's open skies and the smell of Highland heaths. Longed for a return to normal—laughing with his packmates inside the Dragon's Horn, the pub he owned with his brothers-in-arms. All the obnoxious teasing. All the shared meals. All the comforts of home inside the lair he shared with the other Scottish dragon warriors.

Good food.

A soft bed and warm, willing females.

The quick tempers and close comradery he'd taken for granted for too long.

Closing his eyes, Vyroth exhaled a rough breath. He wanted to go home. Wanted to see his brothers' faces instead of picturing them inside his head. Sometimes, if he concentrated hard enough, he heard their voices, listened to the laughter, tasted the Scotch.

The imagined chorus of his packmates sparked in the depths of his mind, urging him on. Told him to keep fighting, never surrender, to be who he'd always been—stubborn to the core, powerful and vicious, a lethal Dragonkind warrior most males avoided at all costs.

Vyroth huffed.

Times had obviously changed.

And no wonder.

He'd been an idiot, believing he could fly into Europe alone. If he managed to escape and return to Scotland, Cyprus would tear a strip off him.

His twin didn't suffer fools lightly.

Neither did his brothers-in-arms.

The brutal males might love him, but that

wouldn't stop them. His pack would convey their displeasure in the old way—with tail, tooth and claw—beating their displeasure into his hide while hammering home the facts.

None of which he could deny.

He *had* been foolish.

He'd let his guard down. Taken a night off. Lost focus and his attention to detail. Though, the female he bedded that evening hadn't complained. She'd received all kinds of his attention. But then, his distraction had been the point. Part of her job. The entire reason she'd been hired—the lead operative in a takedown, one who looked delicious in a short skirt and come-hither smile.

Cursing his stupidity, Vyroth rubbed his hands over his face.

Long stubble scratched over his palms. Forget the soft bed. He needed a shave. The beard made his skin itch and his temper boil. His hair annoyed him too, but long strands falling into his eyes bothered him less than the facial hair. Forced upon him, the scruff grated as much as the river rumbling around him.

He listened to it a moment, detecting the change.

The air cooled a degree. Fog rolled in, curling over the tops of his bare feet.

Vyroth clenched his teeth. Dawn must be on the horizon. The subterranean river streaming around his island always cooled at daybreak, bringing a chill so frigid Vyroth wondered at the location of the fortress sitting above him.

A country other than the Czech Republic?

Had the bastard brought him further north?

Into a region he didn't know?

All good questions. Ones Vyroth wanted answered. Too bad he couldn't recall. Hit with a powerful tranquilizer, he'd been incoherent for the trip. He kept trying to remember, but memory was a tricky thing. His mind kept moving the target, making him question what was real and what he'd imagined. All he knew for sure was that he'd woken up underground—messed up and alone, with a huge hole in his memory.

Fighting a shiver, Vyroth watched the fog thicken. He glanced toward the edge of his platform and the river. Raising fast. Frothing over the edges of his island. Two hundred and fifty yards between him and the steel door on the opposite shore.

He'd attempted the crossing more than once.

Once should've been enough. Burnt skin, sapped strength, the rapid drain of his magic (along with near drowning) had been the result. He stared at the river, then at the door, wondering if he should try it again. Wondering if—

Rapid tapping interrupted his musing, coming through the wall behind him.

Vyroth rolled to his feet. Uneven stone beneath his bare feet, he stood in the center of his island and listened to the message. A series of short raps interspaced by long scrapes. Morse Code, a favorite of Humankind's.

His chest went tight.

Thank fuck.

His mystery friend was back.

He hadn't heard anything all night. The absence felt like weeks. He might not know who stood on the opposite side of the wall, but Vyroth thanked the Goddess for him every day. The intermittent interactions kept him tethered to reality, providing clarity in the midst of insanity.

"You there?"

Calling on what little magic remained, he reached

out with his mind. A rock clip broke away from the jagged side wall. Marshalling his strength, he propelled the small stone with magic and a murmur, rapping it against stone, answering the unknown male's call. *"Here."*

"Okay?"

"Still alive, less than well."

"Haven't fed you yet?"

"No... you?"

"Female just left. I fought to keep her, but..."

"No luck?"

"Took five guards."

Vyroth smiled. *"Kill any?"*

"One. A second's in rough shape."

Good. Bloody bastards. The guards deserved what they got. *"Recharged?"*

"Low energy female, but got enough." A pause, then more forceful tapping. *"Feeling better. Stronger."*

"Good." He closed his eyes, happy for the male, fearful for himself. *"Not sure feeding me is in the cards."*

"Positive thinking."

Vyroth snorted. Two months of positive thinking hadn't gotten him anywhere. He was tired of—

A whisper of sound rolled across the surface of the water.

Pebble poised to strike granite, Vyroth stilled. Coaxing his weakened dragon half to life, he sent his senses searching. His eyes narrowed. Aye, definitely... movement in front of his cell door.

"Hold on." Cocking his head, Vyroth listened harder.

Beeping sounded.

The energy shield powered down.

Soft and light, footsteps paused outside his door. He tapped a rapid, *"Someone's here. Gotta go."*

"Good luck," his friend tapped.

"Later."

Loosing the stone, Vyroth let it fall and shifted to the back of his island, into the shadows. The move wasn't much, barely enough to protect him. But until he laid eyes on the intruder—determined the extent of the threat—something was better than nothing.

Gaze riveted on the door, he crouched, making himself a smaller target. Blood rush whispered in his ears as he listened. A muffled thud. A low curse. Steel groaned against metal. The locking mechanism began to turn. Too weak to fight, left with few defenses, he watched in helpless fascination as the heavy bar lifted and the cell door began to open.

2

___

The quiet rasp across concrete caught Nicole Biscayne's attention. Curled up next to the cinderblock wall on the other side of her prison cell, she controlled her breathing and stayed still. Maybe, if she feigned sleep, whoever stood outside the bars would go away. Forget she existed. Leave her to die in peace.

Whatever. Call it what you will.

Didn't matter how it happened. All she wanted was to be left alone.

Attention inside the dragon lair meant all kinds of things.

Most of them bad.

She'd learned the hard way. At first, she hadn't understood. Now, she knew everything—about Dragonkind and the secret world dragon warriors inhabited.

Incredible, really.

Going unnoticed in human society, keeping such a massive secret from billions of people, took real skill. The kind she didn't want to think about, but really, what else did she have to do? She had nothing but time—to go over everything from the beginning. To mull over her kidnapping. To rummage through the details, all the things she should've done differently. To wish for a quick death, instead of the slow one she now suffered.

Montgomery believed placing her in a dingy prison cell deep underground would break her. Nicole fought every day to prove him wrong. Stay even. Be strong. Never give up.

Not that he cared about her mantras. He kept turning the screws, taking away more and more.

Soft bed in a clean, sunlit room—gone.

Fancy clothes and expensive jewelry—taken away.

Nutritious food replaced by scant portions of bread and water.

The clawing scrape came again.

A hushed voice followed. "Nicole."

Her fingers curled against the thin blanket. *Go away.* Self-preservation screamed it. Her muscles tensed, echoing the sentiment. *Go away, go away... please, please, just go away.*

"Come, *ma petite*," the intruder said, French accent so soothing it tugged at her tension.

Fighting the pull, she concentrated on his voice. French from France, not from Quebec, Canada. Not Cajun or Acadian either. She knew American accents. Had hopscotched all over the country growing up. Spent over a year in the bayous of Louisiana, where creole lived and breathed. The richness of consonants rolling over smooth vowels directed the geography. So too did unmistakable infusion of European arrogance, the assumption of obedience prevalent in his undertone.

"Nicole." The edge of impetrate in his voice drew

her focus. "I know you are frightened, *ma belle*, but I am here to help."

Nicole opened her eyes and stared at the scarred wall. Fingernails. All those scratches had been made by *fingernails*. The desperate clawing of prisoners who'd endured the cell before her.

"Help?" The moment the word left her parched throat, Nicole regretted it. He was using the oldest ruse in the book. Imploring her, feigning concern, to get a reaction. "Tell Montgomery to go to hell."

"I am not here for him," the stranger said. "Come, darling... *petit déjeuner*. Apple slices, an orange, boiled eggs. All for you."

Food... real *food*, instead of crust of bread and dirty water. Her mouth started to water. "You're part of Montgomery's crew."

"Not by choice." A pause, then, "My name is Lapier. My master, Nian, was attacked and killed six months ago."

"And they took you?"

"*Oui.*"

Struggling up onto one elbow, she looked over her shoulder.

Crouched in the shadows outside her cell door, little more than a phantom in the dark, he slipped a bowl between steel bars. Ceramic clinked against the concrete floor.

Her empty stomach growled, and Nicole moved.

Starving herself wasn't the answer. An offer of food couldn't—and shouldn't—be ignored. She needed to regain her strength. Otherwise, she'd never get out of Montgomery's underground maze alive.

Muscles aching, Nicole wrapped the thin blanket around her shoulders and crawled to the side of her bare mattress. Fighting nausea, she slipped her legs over the edge. Cold concrete chilled her bare feet. She stood and, ignoring her trembling limbs, shuffled toward the bowl... and the stranger who'd yet to move.

Mistrustful, eyes glued to him, she crouched five feet away. She didn't want him to reach through the bars and grab her, but... the food. She needed the bowl. Reaching out, she grasped the bowl with her fingertips and dragged it toward her.

The sweet smell of a peeled orange reached her.

Tears welled in her eyes.

"*Pauvre petite*," he whispered, the ache in his voice dulling his accent. "Eat, *ma belle*. Eat it all. I'll wait."

Shoving apple in her mouth, Nicole ate fast, filling her cheeks, swallowing slices barely chewed. Mouth full, she rasped, "Water?"

Lapier set a lidless bottle inside the bars.

Hand shaking, she drank deep, then went back to the first true meal she'd had in over a week. Finishing the last egg, she drank more, then glanced at Lapier. "He lets you roam free?"

"To a point." Sitting yogi style, Lapier pushed a stack of clothing between the bars. "I am watched, but as a Numbai, Montgomery believes me cowed."

"Numbai?"

"I'm not human, Nicole. I see to the care and feeding of Dragonkind. As long as I do my job and am not out of view overlong, the warriors here pay me little attention."

She'd heard of the Numbai, but had never see one. His shrouded silhouette said different, *other*—pointed ears, sharper than normal facial features, an unnatural glimmer in his dark eyes.

Setting the empty bowl aside, she reached for the pile of clothes. Her fingers shuffled through the fabric

—jeans, long-sleeved tee and warm, zip-up sweatshirt, running shoes with thick socks shoved inside on top. "What price for the meal and clothes?"

His winged eyebrows quirked.

"You didn't come down here out of the kindness of your heart."

"Debatable."

"What do you want, Lapier?"

"I need you to escape."

"I'm on board."

He chuckled. "I bet, but—"

"I hate *buts*. I always end up with the short end of the stick."

"Listen carefully," he said, all business, as though about to impart state secrets. "What I need for you to do is dangerous. You must follow my instructions to the letter."

Dread clawed through her. "What is it?"

"You must do exactly as I say, Nicole—agreed?"

"I'm not agreeing to anything until I know what it is."

His mouth curved. "I've always had a soft spot for clever females."

"Lapier," she gritted between clenched teeth, patience running thin.

He shuffled closer to the bars. "There is a warrior imprisoned here. He grows weaker by the day. Without a female, he will die. He must feed, and you—"

"No."

"Nicole..." His voice, so full of understanding, beseeched her. "He is a good male from an honorable pack. He will not hurt you the way Montgomery does."

Her stomach clenched. Nausea rolled, threatening

her recent meal. Another man. Another unwelcome foray into her personal space. More humiliation and pain.

"I can't." Goosebumps pebbled her skin. "Lapier... I can't."

"You must, *ma belle*. He is a strong male with powerful magic. A good feeding will restore him to full strength. The second his dragon half returns, he'll break free and take you with him."

Clutching the bundle of clothes, she backed away from the bars.

"It's the only way you'll ever see the light of day again."

"But Montgomery—"

"Has gone hunting." Up on his knees, Lapier curled his hands around the bars. "He will not return before nightfall. Could be even longer. You will have all day with Vyroth. Be brave, Nicole. Feed him, make him strong again, and you'll be free to go home."

"Home," she whispered, picturing her younger sister and the busy scrapyard her father managed in Savannah.

"Yes, *ma belle... home*."

Squeezing her eyes closed, Nicole shook her head. Freedom instead of death. Fresh air instead of a prison cell. Home instead of here. How could she pass up the opportunity?

"You're sure he won't hurt me?"

"Vyroth's been denied sustenance for two months." Releasing a breath, Lapier withdrew lock-picking tools from his back pocket. "I won't lie to you. He'll be hungry... very, very hungry."

"So dangerous."

"Only if you allow him to be."

"What does that mean?"

"You are the one connected to the Meridian, source of all living things," Lapier said, long, elegant hands working to pick the lock. "You control the flow of energy and, thereby, him. As long as Vyroth's being fed, he will respect the pace you set. Hold tight to that control, Nicole, give him only what you can spare, and you will survive."

"Terrific," she said, yanking on the clothes. "Why me? Why not one of the other women being held here?"

"The others are too well guarded above stairs, and also..."

"Also?"

"You're high energy."

She frowned. "High energy?"

"Rarest of the rare, hooked directly into the Meridian. You possess the most powerful energy I have ever seen."

"The reason Montgomery took me."

"And refuses to let you go," he said, eyes on the lock. "No matter how difficult you've become."

"Asshole."

"No bigger one around." He hummed as the lock clicked and the padlock swung open. "Come. Time is short. I have left everything you need outside his cell. I must get back before any of the guards notice I am gone."

"Where is he being held?"

"Take a right at the end of the corridor, then a left into the next." Yanking the lock from its mooring, Lapier swung the cell door wide. "Third door on the right."

Zipping the hoodie, Nicole inched past him,

leaving the cell. Relief coursed through her. Hope. A way out. She could be well on her way to being *free*.

Lapier held out a slip of paper.

"What's that?" she asked, taking the paper.

"The code to the electronic keypad outside his cell."

Nodding, she slid it into her back pocket.

"One other thing, *ma petite*."

She turned to look at him.

"I need you to take this," he said, holding out a computer memory stick. "And give it to Vyroth."

"Incriminating files?"

"Videos."

"What—"

"The drive is encrypted, but Vyroth will know what to do once the files are open. Whom to contact. Where to send the information."

Taking the memory stick, she tucked it into the front pocket of her jeans.

"It's important, Nicole. Do not lose it. Many lives depend on it."

"I'll give it to him," she whispered, an odd urge coming over her. She didn't question it. She went with instinct and, stepping close, wrapped her arms around Lapier. "What about you?"

"I'll be fine," he said, hugging her back, giving her a squeeze. "Now, go."

She held onto him harder. "Thank you."

"Go, *ma belle*. Do as I ask. See to Vyroth."

Nicole clung for a moment, then did what he wanted and let go.

Standing in the middle of the corridor outside the open cell door, she watched him disappear into the darkness, remembering his instructions. Right, then left, third door along the corridor. Even in the gloom, his cell wouldn't be hard to find, but...

Could she do it?

Could she feed him?

Nicole knew the drill. She'd been forced to feed Montgomery in the beginning. The pain had nearly killed her. No surprise, really. She'd fought him every step of the way, shutting him out, figuring out fast that if she concentrated, she could deny Montgomery what he desired—the energy contained inside her. But as she made her way down the gloomy corridor, Nicole knew she wouldn't be able to deny Vyroth. Not if she wanted to escape Montgomery's cruelty.

She'd already tried (and failed) more times than she cared to count, so...

Nothing for it.

She needed to buck up. Fear had its place, but not here. She must be bold. Feeding Vyroth was a means to an end. The price of freedom, just like purchasing a plane ticket home.

Rounding a corner, she crept down the second hallway. Stone walls, lots of closed doors, steel bars locked in place. No voices or sounds coming from behind them, but... strange. The sound of rushing water seemed to be everywhere—under her feet, behind the walls, overhead—and yet, the flagstones underfoot remained dry.

Must be an underground river.

Not that it mattered.

Her current environment was little more than an impediment in need of scaling.

"Left, left," she muttered, jogging on her tiptoes. "The next left, then—"

There.

Up ahead. An intersection with only two ways to go—left or right.

She veered left into a long hallway. Her palms started to sweat as she spotted the third door and the supplies piled beside it. Now or never. Time to decide. Attempt to find a way out on her own, or enter the dragon's den and pray she survived.

3

———

Cloaked by shadows, Vyroth stayed still as the door to his cell swung open. The gaping hole remained black, without movement or light, depriving him of details. He called on what remained of his magic. Weak, but coherent, his dragon half rose to the challenge.

His night vision sparked.

Not strongly.

Hardly at all.

Just enough to provide a blurry outline of a person in the dark. Small of stature. Light of frame. A new scent broke through the smell of water and must.

Crouched at the back of his platform, Vyroth's nostrils flared. The tang of orange, the sweetness of apples and—

Female.

The pit of his stomach dropped.

He inhaled again to make sure. Could be a trick of the mind. Could be the deprivation talking. Could be a sick trick designed by his captor, but... aye. Without a doubt. A *female* stood outside in the corridor.

Riveted to the harried shadow, he watched her pile things by the door. With a soft grunt, she grabbed what looked like a rope. A scraping sound broke over the rollicking river as she backed into the cell, dragging something. The lines became clear. Vyroth sucked in a breath. A small boat. She was slowing pulling a narrow canoe closer to the shoreline opposite him.

He ran his gaze over her.

Dark hair bound in a thick braid. Round arse pointed in his direction. He couldn't see her face, but... goddess. All that energy. Power sparkled in the electric blue aura surrounding her. Gorgeous color, vibrant and intense. Beauty personified. A high energy female so potent she made his skin prickle from five hundred feet away.

Ravaged by need, his dragon half rose to greet her.

Saliva pooled his mouth.

His muscles cramped.

Watching her work, Vyroth pushed to his feet.

Out of breath, chest rising and falling fast, she stopped when she cleared the frame. Dropping the rope, she skirted the canoe and checked the corridor. He knew it stood empty. She wanted to be sure, looking one way, then the other, before reaching for the door.

The heavy panel swung closed.

A second before the steel edges hit the frame, she softened its landing. A gentle bump, but no noise as she turned away, leaving the door unlocked.

Vyroth's mouth curved. Powerful. Smart. Beautiful, with her smooth skin, full mouth, and dark lashes. The desperate need to see the color of her eyes overwhelmed him. Unable to stop himself, he stepped out of the shadows.

Her head came up.

Light brown eyes collided with his over the surface of the water.

She stopped short. A slight tremor in her hands, she raked long bangs out of her eyes. "Vyroth?"

The tentativeness in her tone carried, clawing through him.

Christ. She was scared... with good reason. Given his condition, any female with half a brain would be. He needed to reassure her, quickly, before she turned tail and ran.

"Aye, lass," he said, smoothing his growl, keeping his voice gentle.

"I'm coming across, but..." she paused.

He held his breath. "But?"

"I have conditions."

Smart female. His desire for her grew by the second. "Tell me."

"You don't touch me."

"*Tazleiah*," he said, calling her *braveheart* in Dragonese. "I won't be able tae—"

"Until I say. You don't touch me until I say." She pushed the canoe forward. The bow slipped into the water. "I know you're hungry, and I'll feed you, but I have to control it."

Hands curled into fists, desperate for her to start paddling, he stared at her.

"Also," she said, piling on, threatening his control. "You take me with you when you break out. I won't stay here. I don't get left behind for any reason—understood?"

No hardship.

An easy deal to make.

A high energy female was too valuable to leave behind. "Agreed."

At the stern, ready to launch, she looked at him

across the expanse. "Back of the platform. On your knees, hands on the nape of your neck."

An accepted inmate position.

She'd seen far too many prison shows.

His mouth curved at the thought.

"Vyroth," she said, a warning in her tone.

Riveted onto the promise of her, his dragon half acquiesced, obeying without argument, unlocking his muscles, allowing him to move. Hunger out of control, dying to touch her, he knelt on rough stone. Gaze locked on her, he watched her settle into the stern seat and push away from the bank.

The paddle rose and fell.

Steady strokes.

Measured pace.

Water dripped off the end, splattering the gunnels, driving him crazy with each splashing slice of the paddle.

She paused mid-stroke, holding the wooden blade over the water.

Playing the game, he bowed his head and raised his arms. His hands found the back of his head. Chin tucked into his chest, Vyroth watched her from beneath his lashes, control so thin he knew he couldn't do what she asked. The second she landed on dry ground, his dragon would slip the leash and, without mercy, take control of her.

4

____

Working against the current, Nicole controlled the canoe. The bow sliced through the churning chop. The strength of the river pushed her off course. She upped the pace, keeping each stroke of the paddle strong. Not an easy feat given she had one eye on Vyroth. The closer she got to his shoreline, the more nervous she became.

He was a big man.

Much larger than Montgomery.

At least six and a half feet tall, probably taller. Muscular arms. Wide shoulders. Lean hips and long, strong legs. On his knees, arms raised, elbows bent, he still looked powerful. A chill swept over her skin. Goosebumps rose. No doubt about it. If he decided to break the deal, touch her before she was ready, she wouldn't be able to stop him.

Halfway across, she dipped, then angled the paddle, steering her course while contemplating another. She still had time. With a slight adjustment, she could swing the bow around and turn back.

She hesitated, blade in the water, grip on the wooden shaft painful.

Even from a hundred feet away, Nicole knew he

wasn't safe. She saw the tension in his frame. Sensed his mood as he eyed her beneath his lashes. Need rolled off him in waves, heating the air, yet somehow, deepening her chill.

Lapier hadn't lied.

Vyroth was something altogether different.

Nothing like the guys she encountered in the castle.

Even weak with hunger, he exuded a power so potent she wondered if she'd survive him. Not that she had a choice. The Numbai was right. She'd never make it out of the underground prison alone.

Navigation wasn't one of her strengths.

She'd get turned around by the labyrinthine corridors... and lost wasn't something she wanted to be when the guards showed up. Nicole understood the routine, had listened to the thump of footfalls as patrols passed her cell. Heard the quiet jeers. Absorbed the insulting barbs. Pretended to ignore them all.

The memory surfaced like acid in her veins.

Anything... *anything*... was better than staying here.

Even facing off with Vyroth.

Resetting her courage, she started paddling again. Swift strokes learned in the bayou took her closer to the dock. Carved from stone, the small jetty jutted into the river. Choosing to land starboard side, she brought the canoe in for a smooth landing. Fast running water pushed her sideways. The gunnel bumped against stone, rocking her as she reached for the rope.

"Hold on a sec," she said, tying the bow off on a dock cleat. "I'll just—"

Huge hands grabbed her.

She gasped.

The unmoored stern swung wide as Vyroth lifted her out of her boat. He wrapped her hard against him.

Back to his chest, Nicole panicked as he pulled her against him. "Stop!"

He growled, sounding more animal than human.

She reared to loosen his hold. Why? No clue. The effort was worse than useless. He had her now. Even half-starved, he was too much for her to handle, far too strong. Breaking away now was an impossibility.

No way out.

Zero possibility of success.

She needed to stop fighting him. Find another way to tamp down his aggression.

"Vyroth…"

Blocking her attempt to turn and face him, he pushed his hand beneath her top. His palm ghosted over her skin. Inside of his forearm pressed to her belly, his fingers curled over her hipbone. Fear skittered through her as he anchored her with one hand and cupped her throat with the other. With a snarl, he set his mouth against her nape. Three points of connection—throat, hip, nape. She knew the drill, tried to hold the line, to slow him down, but—

Heat rolled through her veins.

Something clicked inside her.

Her vision blurred as the cosmic strings holding her together frayed.

Energy rushed through the holes.

Holding her tight, he connected, tunneling straight into her stream. She heard the rush in her ears, felt the jolt as her body bucked, heard him groan as he got his first taste.

"Slowly… slow," she rasped, realigning her senses, narrowing the flow, funneling the energy. "Vyroth, gently… gently."

"Mine. Mine."

"Gently."

"More," he moaned, the sharp edge of his teeth against her skin.

"In a minute." Taking a shaky breath, she forced her muscles to loosen. Her spine softened. Energy began to flow smooth instead of jagged. He drank deep. She let him, relaxing into him, forcing him to take her weight, blunting her edges, inviting him to do the same. "Take what I give you first."

Controlling the flow, she fed him a steady stream. The more she gave, the gentler he became. His grip on her changed, moving from desperate and brutal to tender and caressing. The combination caused a chain reaction. Fear faded. Bone deep contentment took its place, bumping her into a pleasure so profound, Nicole didn't fight it.

Taut muscles unwound.

Relaxation untethered her.

Closing her eyes, she drifted into his heat and, turning her head, nestled in. His mouth jumped to her temple. The intensity increased. Nicole leaned into the stream, cranking the connection wide open, all fear of him gone.

Cradling her now, he mumbled something.

Her lashes fluttered open, then fell. "Hmm?"

He murmured again.

Oh. Name. He wanted to know her name. Trying to make her mouth work, she attempted to tell him. Nothing came out. She tried again. "Nicole... Niki."

"Niki... beautiful," he whispered, turning her in his arms.

Soft bristles ghosted over her cheek.

Feeling drugged, she buried her hands in his dark hair. He nipped the underside of her chin. Shivers raked her as he dipped his head and set his mouth against the corner of hers. His teeth grazed her bottom lip. She tipped her chin up, offering her throat, giving him greater access.

"Niki, no." Working his fingers into her braid, he brought her mouth back to his.

She turned her head away. "No kissing."

"Sex?"

"No."

He grunted, but didn't argue.

Dropping to his knees, he wrapped her tighter against him. Her back touched down on a smooth patch of stone. He gave her his weight. She accepted it without question. Had he demanded, used his strength, forced her to submit, she would've fought him. She didn't know any other way, but Vyroth steered a new course. Instead of hurting, he comforted, cajoling without words, coaxing her to give more, the draw so gentle she forgot to be cautious.

Her mind blanked.

Her body softened.

The stream of energy flared, widening until he had it all.

Vyroth moaned and licked over her pulse point. Bliss skipped down her spine. Overcome by sensation, bathed in his heat, Nicole ignored the danger and drew him closer, self-preservation a distant memory as she followed him into oblivion.

5

Vyroth surfaced through mental fog, coming up through thick layers of sleep a little at a time. Awareness nudged him. He cracked his eyes open. His lids slid closed again. He didn't want to wake up yet. He was warm for the first time in... hellfire, seemed like forever.

He couldn't remember when he'd been so relaxed.

Probably years ago. Before it all went bad.

The thought drifted, insisting he roll over and get the hell out. Away from the danger.

Danger.

Danger.

Danger.

The word spun inside his mind, breaking through the drift of warm and comfortable. Yawning, Vyroth rubbed his eyes. What seemed to be the problem? He was relaxed and well-rested, fingertips tingling as magic hummed in his veins and—

His brows collided.

Bloody hell. He wasn't hungry anymore.

The realization jolted through him. Full. He felt *full.* No hunger pangs. Zero body drain. Dragon half awake, waiting for him to come around, warning him he needed to move... and do it now.

Vyroth forced his eyes open. Fuzzy brain. Poor visual acuity. Slow reflexes. Struggling to get his bearings, he blinked the blur away. Black granite ceiling. Thick vein of white quartz cutting through the dark stone. The pounding rush of water sliced through the mental fog. The warm nest of blankets he lay inside registered next.

Flexing his fingers, he counted all his limbs.

His dragon half stretched, uncoiling inside him.

Magic pooled in his palms as power snaked through him, raising the fine hairs on his nape. The blur impairing his vision disappeared. His senses went from sluggish to razor-sharp. Inhaling deep, Vyroth exhaled on a growl. So good. So bloody good. Having gone without for so long, nothing felt better than—

A wisp of warm air ghosted over his throat.

He stilled, becoming aware of the soft body tucked against his. Trying to remember what happened, Vyroth glanced down. Head half buried in his chest, half beneath the blanket, he couldn't see much, just a wealth of thick, dark hair.

Nicole.

Thank the goddess.

She was still with him. Hadn't escaped after he fed, while he recovered.

Awe whispered through him. A high energy female. A rare find for a Dragonkind male. He'd never seen, never mind touched one before. No wonder he felt so full.

Afraid to wake her, but unable to resist, he touched her hair. So soft. Silky smooth. A long curtain, dark and lovely. Sometime during the day, he'd unbraided the unruly mass. Now, the thick strands lay everywhere—all over his chest, tangled beneath his chin, in his beard, and now, between his fingers.

Shifting through the beautiful strands, he drew the blanket down, revealing her face. Still asleep. Breathing even and sure. So relaxed she lay pliant and trusting in his arms. His mouth curved. His wee angel —the female brave enough to confront his dragon half and save his life.

His chest tightened.

Vyroth swallowed past the emotion. Thank the goddess for Nicole. Without her, he never would've made it. His need had been desperate, his dragon half greedy during the first feeding. She weathered his storm, controlled the connection, forced him to slow down, preventing him from taking too much too fast.

Brave female. A bewitching sprite with a strong spirit.

Curling into her, he brushed the dark hair away from her face. With a sigh, she snuggled in, seeking more of his heat. He gave it without reservation, calling on his magic. Cold air heated. A warm bubble formed around the blankets.

Ones he didn't remember conjuring.

His dragon half was in fine form.

Attuned to her needs, his beast provided without being asked, assuring her comfort as Vyroth fed and... praise be, she'd done beautifully. Given him all he needed. Fed him so well, the power he took for granted, but hadn't sensed in months, bubbled in his veins, ready to be used.

Closing his eyes, he experienced the fullness of it.

Nicole was power personified. A firecracker in an explosive wee package. Such a gift he didn't know who to thank first—her or the one who sent her.

Turning onto his side, he pushed deeper into her embrace. "Niki."

Legs and arms tangled around him, she mumbled something.

"*Tazleiah*... beautiful lass," he whispered in her ear. "Wake up."

A pucker marred her brow. She growled at him.

Vyroth stifled a chuckle. She was an adorable grump. So pretty in slumber he wanted to stay put, give her what she needed and let her sleep. Or mayhap, kiss her awake. His body stirred, liking the suggestion, reacting to the promise of her.

Vyroth tightened his control.

He wanted the kiss, yearned to taste her, but not yet. Mayhap, not for a while. Nicole wasn't ready. Her denial earlier came with a message. He heard her loud and clear. She needed time. Time to heal. Time to come to know and accept him. Time to understand he was nothing like the bastard who'd clipped her wings and stolen her freedom.

Rubbing her back, he jostled her. "Niki?"

"No."

He nipped her ear.

"Go." Angling her head, she pressed her face into his throat. "Away."

Slurred words. He picked up her meaning just the same.

"Cannae, baby," he said, keeping his voice low, lamenting her exhaustion. His fault. He'd taken too much. If he'd been in the safety of his own bed—anywhere but here—he would've left her in peace, but not today. "We need tae move."

Her eyelashes fluttered open, then shut.

Stroking her back, he waited, rousing her a little at

a time. "There's a good lass. Open your eyes. Look at me."

She grumbled a complaint, but listened. Light brown eyes surrounded by dark lashes met his.

Groggy, not quite tracking, she remained relaxed in his arms. Her compliance wouldn't last. She was too strong a female to abide weakness and accept his comfort for long. Which meant the second her mind cleared, she'd move away. Put space between him and her. Seek to protect herself while she plotted the next step.

Vyroth understood, but didn't want her going anywhere.

His dragon half agreed.

Sometime during the day, his beast made a decision. Entrenched now, the stubborn bastard dug in, marking Nicole as his mate. Vyroth hadn't recognized her on sight—so hungry he failed to see anything but her abundant energy—but his dragon half had known from the start, and now...

Vyroth drew a deep breath.

Hellfire. His *mate*. Here in a hellhole designed to cage and keep him.

The idea nearly undid him. What if he hadn't been captured? What if he'd managed to escape before she reached him? If not for the ambush, he never would've met Nicole, wouldn't be holding her, wouldn't know the pleasure of being truly full for the first time in his life.

She stirred, legs moving restless against his. "I'm not dead."

"Pardon?"

"You didn't kill me," she said, sounding surprised.

"Nay, *Tazleiah*, but I took more than I should've. You'll feel the effects for a while." Stoking the hair away from her face, he caressed her, enjoying the softness of her skin. "Normally, I'd let you sleep, but we cannae stay here much longer."

"Guards?"

"Just walked past."

She jerked in his arms. "The door. Vyroth, I didn't close it all the wa—"

"I closed it hours ago, lass. Set the electronic keypad too."

"But..." she trailed off, frowning. "If the force field's up, then we'll never get out of here."

"The guards are young. Inexperienced. None noticed it was deactivated."

Planting her elbow, she twisted to look over her shoulder. Her gaze travelled past the island edge, over the river to the door. "How? How did you—"

"Magic, an ability inherent in my kind."

"I know."

Something about her tone set him on edge. "You find that out the hard way?"

A muscle flexed along her jaw.

"Niki," he said, prompting her, a sick feeling in the pit of his stomach. "Did he hurt you?"

She looked away.

Cupping her cheek, he brought her back. "Look at me, lass."

A sheen in her eyes, she met his gaze, hers defiant. "It's none of your business."

"Not true. Everything about you is now my business. The moment you entered my cage, you became mine tae protect."

She shook her head.

"Aye, Niki... everything."

"I want out." Her breath hitched. His heart broke,

shattering at what he saw in her eyes—the pain and confusion... the terror. "I want to go home."

"I'll get you out. Home may have tae wait for a while."

"What—why?"

"I'll explain Dragonkind to you later. Right now, we need tae move."

"The guards," she whispered. "They just passed, so we have an hour before—"

"They make another round. Aye, lass, I know."

Looking everywhere but at him, she shoved at the blankets. "You're okay now?"

"Fully charged," he said, electric current crackling along his spine, naught but a quick command away. "Thank you, Niki."

With a nod, she shuffled backward, away from him and...

So it began.

The withdrawal. Her abandonment of him as she re-established a safe distance.

Shrugging off the blankets, he sat up, pulling her with him. "Can you walk?"

"I don't know." Legs curled beneath her, she pressed her palm into the floor. "I haven't had enough to eat for a while and—"

"What?"

Nicole brushed off his aggressive tone. "It's not a big deal."

Not a big deal. Had she lost her bloody mind?

"The bastard's been starving you?" The need to kill something roared through him. "I'm going to rip his face off and shove it up his arse."

"I'd like to see that," she said, a smile playing at the corners of her mouth. Brushing long bangs out of her eyes, she wobbled as she stood up.

"But for now, can we go? I'm shaky, but able to move."

Shaky was normal. Only natural after the hours she spent feeding him.

Rolling to his feet beside her, he lifted her into his arms.

"Vyroth."

"Relax," he murmured, striding across the platform toward the dock. "The moment you're strong enough, I'll put you down, let you walk. Right now, I'm getting us the hell out of here."

Nicole didn't argue, but as she curled her arms around his neck, allowing him to carry her, Vyroth prayed escape would be that simple. He didn't like the look of the river. Late-afternoon always saw it rise. Now it tumbled over the edge of the platform, throwing the smell of brine into the air.

His focus narrowed on the canoe.

Small boat.

Raging river.

Bad odds.

The boat looked unsafe. Completely unstable. Far too tiny, hardly big enough to hold Nicole, never mind him.

Tossed by a strong current, the canoe bobbed as he moved along the stone quay. The closer he got, the more his unease grew. He considered shifting into dragon form, but...

The shift posed a different set of problems.

The opposite bank was too narrow, the angled wall too close. He wouldn't be able to land. His wings would tangle, take him off balance and—

"What's wrong?"

"I'm not a strong swimmer." A tight grip on her, he stopped beside the canoe. Trying not to look at the water, he crouched and forced himself to set her down inside the bobbing death trap.

"Is that a dragon thing or just you?"

"Me," he said, stalling, not wanting to get into the boat with her. "Most Dragonkind males donnae like water, but tolerate it well enough, but I'm different."

"How?"

"I'm a lightning dragon," he said, giving her half an answer, not wanting to admit the whole truth. No one but his brothers knew salt water could kill him. The fewer who knew, the better for him.

"An electrical issue?"

"Aye."

"Okay. Well..." Settling on her knees, she shifted her weight, balancing the boat. "I'll keep it steady."

Nicole reached for a paddle.

"Donnae bother, lass. We willnae need it."

She threw him a skeptical look.

He grabbed the gunnel. "Ready?"

"Set. Go."

Under normal circumstances, her quip would've made him laugh, but not now. With his heart thumping and fear out in full force, Vyroth didn't even smile. He took a fortifying breath instead and prepared to hop aboard, praying he made it across the expanse before his phobia took over and capsized them both.

6

———

The canoe rocked as Vyroth climbed in. Nicole gripped the gunnels so hard her hands hurt as she battled to keep the boat steady. A difficult endeavor. He was a big guy, wide-shouldered, muscular, much, much taller than her. Watching him move, curiosity got the better of her. She almost asked him if he was taller than six-foot-five. She wanted to ask him about his eyes. Mismatched—one electric blue, one pale purple. An odd combination. Then again, everything about Dragonkind seemed strange to her.

The magic.

The ability to shift from human to dragon form.

The fact his kind remained hidden on a planet populated by human beings. Someone had to have noticed by now.

Nicole chewed on her bottom lip. So many questions. Most of them about him. His accent pointed to Scotland. His size and strength veered toward brutality. The way he handled her indicated gentle. The dichotomy seemed impossible. A mystery to be solved and, she wanted to ask. Really, she did, but at the last second, veered toward self-preservation and killed her curiosity.

She didn't need to be wondering about him.

Vyroth already took up too much space inside her head.

Nicole breathed out as he finally settled at the stern. He kneeled, mimicking her position, knees to the fiberglass bottom, steadying the small craft, making her even more nervous. He was behind her, able to strike before she reacted... or moved to protect herself. She hated the vulnerability and the way it made her feel. Too much like when—

She squeezed her eyes shut, killing the thought. She refused to think about Montgomery. She couldn't stomach reliving the experience. Couldn't stay calm and do what needed to be done if—

"*Tazleiah*—relax. I willnae hurt you. I would never do that." Vyroth's gentle tone reached out to stroke her. A warm prickle ghosted down her spine. "*Never*, lass."

Unable to release her death grip on the canoe, she turned her head and looked at him from the corner of her eye. His gaze met and held hers. She shivered. He murmured again, something nonsensical, non-words, yet she felt taut muscles give way, relaxing beneath the onslaught of his voice.

Large hands wrapped around the crosspiece, he leaned forward. "Better. Now, unmoor us."

Under some kind of strange spell, she blinked. Mind a bit sluggish, she stared at him. He gestured to the rope. Understanding struck and, reaching forward, she yanked the knot free.

The canoe began to drift.

Nicole reached for a paddle.

She needn't have bothered.

Between one heartbeat and the next, Vyroth took

control. Static electricity crackled around the boat. The bow swung around and, without human propulsion, cut through the choppy surf. Water splashed against the sides. Nicole hung on, watching the opposite shore come closer and closer. In less than half the time it took her to paddle across, the canoe traversed the river.

Water went from deep to shallow.

The bow scraped the bottom, then sliced onto the narrow beach. Smooth, black pebbles dispersed, welcoming the canoe on dry land.

Without being told, Nicole hopped out. Her feet sank ankles deep in round stones. Relief hit her. It felt familiar. Not the pebbles, but the act of disembarking. The muscle memory as she grabbed the bow crosspiece and pulled the canoe further onto the beach. She sighed. Finally, something ordinary and well-known. She'd spent hours in canoes and kayaks. Her dad loved lakes and rivers, along with boats of all kinds. He'd taken her out on day trips all the time, teaching, preaching, ensuring his daughters knew how to be safe on the water.

Wary of the river, Vyroth made his way to the bow and jumped out.

Small stones clattered.

Nicole moved toward the cell door.

She didn't make it.

Grabbing her hand, Vyroth jogged passed her. Her arm straightened. She jolted as he began towing her behind him.

"Hey!"

"I go first, lass... always. I shield you, Niki, not the other way around."

She wanted to argue, but that would be idiotic. She wouldn't escape without him. The castle aboveground had security. Lots of it. And honestly, after a month of misery, having a strong, magic-wielding guy for a shield sounded like a good idea. Still, she refused to be bossed—or towed—around.

Shaking her hand, she tried to break free.

With a huff, he laced his fingers through hers, tightened his grip. "Donnae fight it, lass. You willnae win."

Thick Scottish brogue. Soothing cadence. Her muscles relaxed into acceptance.

Nicole pursed her lips. The man was dangerous. So very *dangerous*. From his size to her unending curiosity about him—everything about him screamed *get away and do it now*.

"I'd like to win," she grumbled. "At least once."

"Some other time."

Vyroth stopped in front of the cell door. Drawing her close, he tilted his head, listening to something. Holding her breath, she listened too. Why? No clue. She couldn't hear a thing, but knew Vyroth could. Of all the information she learned in captivity, a Dragonkind warrior's elevated abilities was one of the hardest to take.

She'd jimmied her bedroom window and climbed out onto the high ledge countless times.

She'd managed to sneak out a side door and across the lawn twice.

She'd snuck up behind one with a knife exactly once.

No success. Little use in trying.

She couldn't hear through solid walls. She couldn't see in the dark. She wasn't nearly strong enough. The assholes had played along, amused by her attempts, allowing her to *almost* escape before dragging her back. Each time, hope had risen only to be dashed.

A terrible trick.

Merciless and cruel.

Psychological warfare at its finest.

"Nicole?"

"Yeah?"

"Stop thinking about it. I can't concentrate with your thoughts inside my head."

"What?" Her voice cracked as her mouth went dry. "You're reading—"

"Your mind? Aye, every word." Giving her hand a squeeze, he glanced down at her. His mismatched eyes began to shimmer. "I'm sorry you suffered. We'll talk about it later, but for now, I need you tae shelve the hurt. Put away the pain. Keep only the next step in your thoughts, lass."

His words made her go hot, then cold.

Dread spiked as something awful occurred her.

Nicole hung onto her tears. She swallowed each one down. No more crying. No more feeling sorry for herself. No more unanswered questions.

She cleared her throat. "Do you think—"

"No," he said, his denial guttural. "He couldn't read you."

"Then why can you?"

"Later, Niki. Let me get us out of here first." His eyes went from shimmer to glow. "But know, he willnae touch you again. The second I find him, the bastard's dead. Clear?"

Throat so tight she couldn't talk, Nicole nodded. Sounded good to her. She wanted Montgomery and his crew dead. The sooner it happened, the safer she would be.

The electronic keypad activated.

Beeping joined the rush of water.

The circular handle turned. A moment later, the steel door creaked open.

Keeping her close, Vyroth peered into the hallway. He looked both ways, then dragged her behind him, out of the cell, into an underground labyrinth teaming with unfriendly Dragonkind.

7

The cell door closed with a quiet click. Eyes trained on the empty hallway, Vyroth murmured a command. The manual locks turned. A soft beep echoed along stone as the electronic keypad reactivated. Less than a second later, the energy shield came back online, setting his teeth on edge.

Holding Nicole's hand, he tucked her close to his side and rechecked his surroundings. Thick stone walls covered in damp. Low ceiling six inches above his head. Nothing but the muted rush of the subterranean river left behind in his cell.

Dragon senses switched to maximum, he listened harder. He blocked out the beat of his heart—and the pounding of Nicole's—searching for trace in the underground prison. Magic curled through his veins. Tiny echoes raised his radar. His sonar kicked in, delivering a grid, mapping the labyrinthine alleys tunneling through solid rock.

Soft pings raised the baseline, intersecting with his dragon half. Sound waves connected inside his head, allowing him to hear *everything*. Faint murmurs of male voices. Faraway beats of steady footfalls. No one in immediate range.

Which meant it was time to decide.

Go right or turn left?

A considerable choice. One he must weigh with care.

Corridors spun out, spidering in all directions. Take the wrong one, and he'd be navigating tight tunnels for hours. Choose the right one, and he'd reach fresh air in less than an hour. Given a choice, he'd choose the faster way. He refused to linger. Couldn't do what he wanted and retaliate—annihilate the enemy, leave a few guards in his wake before leaving Montgomery's lair.

Not with Nicole in tow.

His dragon refused to risk her.

Vyroth agreed with his better half. Nicole had suffered enough. Putting her through more was unthinkable. She might be skeptical, but he hadn't lied. He intended to become her shield. No one would ever force her to do anything against her will again. If he had his way, pain and fear would cease to be a part of her life.

A tall order.

A daunting climb.

But the pain she carried deep inside—along with the little she allowed to surface in her eyes—required the effort. He couldn't fix it. Wasn't foolish enough to believe he could. The bastard had hurt her...badly. He might not know the details yet, but it didn't take a genius to figure out.

Males hurt females all the time.

Dishonorable. Disgusting. An offense Dragonkind treated seriously, death the ultimate punishment for the one committing the crime.

Her reaction to him in the boat told him more than he wanted to acknowledge. Brave wee lass. Her courage humbled him. Hurting, no doubt terrified, she'd come to him. Fed him. Healed him. Allowed him to hold her. Vyroth's throat tightened. *Beloved.* That's what Nicole was—a female to be revered.

Failing her wasn't an option.

To prove his worth, he must provide. Anything she needed. Everything she wanted. All he had to give.

Nicole might not know it yet, but she belonged with him. The bond had formed fast. Lightning quick. Took a split second. Not surprising. Energy-fuse worked that way.

The moment he touched her—tasted her—the magical tendrils sank deep, merging his life force with hers, allowing him to delve into her mind. Thoughts. Desires. Insecurities. Happiness. Sadness. The anxiety she held tight and struggled to let go. He accessed it all without effort, and understood more than she knew.

Something that would become a bone of contention for her.

Guaranteed.

Nicole wasn't a weak female. Her personality matched the power of her connection to the Meridian —source of all living things. Convincing her to stay with him would be challenging. Near impossible. But then, he was a long-odds kind of male, and he had all kinds of time. No matter her fears, she'd come to him...eventually.

The bond between mates was simply too strong to ignore.

She belonged to him now.

His to protect. His to spoil. His to love when she let him.

Vyroth swallowed a growl of satisfaction and,

lacing his fingers with hers, turned right down the dark corridor. Poorly fed light globes bobbed in the seams where ceiling met wall, throwing weak light, casting long shadows. His night vision sparked as he tugged Nicole in his wake. The smell of must and rot rose in the narrow space. Vyroth kept going, using his magic to silence their footfalls.

Quick and quiet was best.

He didn't want to get into a firefight. Protecting Nicole, getting out, was more important than his violent plans for Montgomery. He'd see to those later. After he found a safe place for his female and ensured her comfort. After he called his brothers. After the Scottish pack mobilized and jumped the channel from the Highlands to Europe. But first, he needed to escape the subterranean prison and offer up a location.

The drug had wiped all memory of his arrival clean.

Now, he didn't know where he was—other than underground. Had the bastard brought him to the countryside or imprisoned him beneath city streets? Inside a mountain or under a cathedral? Germany, the Czech Republic or inside Russian borders? Anyone's guess. So first things first—get topside and his bearings before anyone discovered he'd broken out of his cell.

Coming to the end of the corridor, Vyroth stopped. His gaze tracked to a lone cell door. He frowned. Unlike his, the door wasn't solid steel, but rotting wood. Darkened by damp, the planks wouldn't keep a groundhog out...or in. But the sharp buzz of electricity beyond the decay raised his instincts. He sensed a presence in the darkness, a powerful one he couldn't ignore.

He reached for the rusted handle.

Metal clanked.

Nicole brushed up against his arm. "What is it?"

"My neighbor."

"Your what?"

He squeezed her hand in answer and, applying pressure, muscled the door open. Jagged wood teeth scraped along the slimy stone floor. Dipping his head beneath the low lintel, Vyroth entered the cell.

Electricity zipped over his skin and into his veins.

He flexed his free hand. Lightning arced between his fingertips. A pleasant buzz ghosted through him. He breathed in the magic, then focused on the interior. Large room. Wicked-looking steel cage bolted to the floor, ceiling, and walls. Horizontal and vertical rods welded close together, blue arcs of current electrifying the bars.

He glanced at the male imprisoned inside.

Massive male, even bigger than him, and at six-foot-six, Vyroth was no slouch. Muscular build. Huge hands with scarred knuckles. Vicious vibe. Relaxed posture, sitting cross-legged on the cage floor, seemingly unconcern by the intrusion. Brown eyes with pale green outer-rims leveled on him.

Vyroth's mouth curved. Excellent. Exactly what he ordered. A Dragonkind warrior, ready-made and ready to roll.

Tugging Nicole away from the door, he positioned her, back to the wall. "Stay here, lass."

"Vyroth," she whispered, strain in her tone. "Who's that?"

He didn't answer. Hard to do, given he didn't have a name. But he knew the male. Had spent two months talking to him through the wall.

Giving her a reassuring squeeze, he released her hand. "Willnae be but a minute."

Focused on the male, Vyroth approached the cage.

"I wouldn't, asshole."

Interesting accent. A hint of Russian, but something else too.

Vyroth raised a brow. "Nay?"

"Not unless you want to become barbeque."

Amused by the warning, he stopped a foot from the bars. Electricity crackled in welcome, caressing him as he reached out. Rolling to his feet, the male backed away. Vyroth didn't hesitate. Eyes on the male, he grabbed a steel upright. Heat bloomed against his palm. Lightning fractured, arcing over the cage and down his arm, surrounding him in beautiful, blinding, snapping blue light.

Dropping a smooth stone, the warrior stared at the display, drawing a deep breath as Vyroth manipulated the lightning into a ball of energy.

Wonder suffused his expression. "Lightning dragon."

"Aye," Vyroth said, gaze on the male. "You want out of here?"

"Who are you?"

"Vyroth." He tipped his chin, gesturing to the rock wall abutting one side of the cage. "Your next door neighbor."

Watching electricity spike outside the cage, he pointed to his chest. "Tempel."

"From the Belarus pack?"

Tempel nodded. "You're Cyprus's blood brother. From the Scottish pack."

"I am," he said. "Your better half?"

"Earth dragon."

Vyroth's mouth curved. Interesting. No wonder the male was so big. Earth dragons drew energy directly from the planet. Males of that bent tended to be antisocial, lethal when even a little annoyed, and needed to feed less often. Handy, given he didn't want Tempel anywhere near Nicole. Also useful if he possessed a certain subset of earth dragon skills.

"You a digger?"

Tempel nodded. "I burrow."

"Feel like being a team player?"

"What do you think?" Flicking his fingers, he tossed a second stone over his shoulder. "Get me the hell out of here."

Vyroth huffed, but didn't argue. Time wasn't on their side. By his count, he had forty minutes before the foot patrol prowled back around. Having a strong male at his back, one who—by the looks of his scarred hands—knew how to fight was a stellar idea. The fact he knew Tempel from hours of Morse-code conversations simply solidified his conviction.

A new brother-in-arms.

One who would watch his six and fight to protect his female.

Nothing better in the world than making a bad-tempered, vicious new friend.

8

Watching the two men across the cell, Nicole retreated into the back wall. Rough stone scraped her sweatshirt, pressing into her shoulder blades. She welcomed the bite. Anything to ground her as she struggled to keep panic at bay. She'd felt it before. She felt it now, coiling inside her chest, climbing up her throat, threatening to engulf her.

Her breaths came faster.

Her eyes started to sting.

She inhaled deep and exhaled slow. In and out. Slow and steady. The technique usually worked. She needed it to right now. Otherwise, fear would avalanche into overwhelm and drag her under.

In.

Out.

Catch and release.

Slow and steady breaths.

Battling to stay even, Nicole told herself a story. One she hoped found its roots in the truth. Vyroth wouldn't hurt her. He hadn't yet. Despite being Dragonkind, he seemed like a stand-up guy. The kind who would never force a woman to do anything. All points in his favor. Problem was, believing something didn't make it true.

Anything could happen.

Circumstances changed.

Priorities shifted.

Like they were right now as Vyroth upped the ante, adding a new variable to the already complicated tangle inside her head. Her eyes tracked him. She heard every word he exchanged with Tempel, paying strict attention, picking up details, tearing apart nuance, trying to understand. What was Vyroth doing?

Tempel didn't look the least bit friendly.

He looked scary. Tall. Strong. Scarred. Cold, expressionless eyes. Capable of delivering brutality, the kind she never wanted to encounter again.

Ever again.

Her fingers trembled as she fisted her hands. She shouldn't be here. She should be running, not standing where Vyroth left her. Nicole swallowed past the lump in her throat. So why wasn't she?

The question made her even more tense.

The answer came at once.

She couldn't run. Not yet. Her sense of direction sucked. She'd take a wrong turn, make a poor decision, and end up right back where she started—locked down inside a cell with Montgomery breathing down her neck.

So few options. No good solutions.

Much as it pained her, Vyroth meant safety right now, providing a real shot at freedom. He was strong. He possessed skills she couldn't match. He knew his way around the Dragonkind world. All she wanted was out. But as the cage door creaked open and Tempel dipped his head beneath the steel frame and stepped out, thoughts of fleeing intensified.

She slid along the wall toward the door.

"Niki."

She flinched at the sound of Vyroth's voice. Her attention flicked from Tempel to him. Her gaze collided with his mismatched one. She tried to look away. He refused to let her, stopping her unwise flight with intent, shimmering blue and violet eyes.

"He willnae hurt you, lass."

Air hiccupped in her chest. Her breath hitched. "He doesn't touch me... at all—ever."

"I would never do that, *talmina*," Tempel said, tone gruff, undercurrent gentle. "You belong to Vyroth."

"What?"

"Easy assumption, darlin'. His scent is all over you."

Nicole opened her mouth to object.

She closed it again.

No sense clarifying. Little reason to tell him she didn't belong to anyone. Not if it meant Tempel stayed away from her. Vyroth was one thing. She'd spent the day with him. Other than nagging fatigue, she was none the worse for wear. Something intuition told her she wouldn't be able to say if Tempel got ahold of her.

Brown eyes rimmed with green met hers.

Tempel raised a brow.

Nicole suppressed a shiver.

"Come here, lass."

Her attention snapped back to Vyroth. She shook her head. No way. She wasn't getting any closer to Tempel.

Steadying her with his gaze, Vyroth held out his hand, palm up.

"We need to go."

"We will... once you come tae me."

"Vyroth—"

"*Tazleiah*, trust me. Just a wee bit further."

Baby steps. He was asking for *baby steps*. Give a little, be rewarded. Nicole recognized the ploy. Had learned all about it in school—Psychology 101. Building trust took time. Was nuanced and layered. Happened in increments, little by little, until a bond grew through shared experience.

Clever.

Terrible and manipulative given the timeline mattered.

Vyroth flicked his fingers.

She pursed her lips. "Stubborn."

"Aye." Amusement sparked in his eyes. "One of my better qualities."

"Debatable," she said, pushing away from the wall.

Time to give up. Arguing wouldn't help the cause. She wouldn't win, and standing around wasn't smart. The guards made their rounds once every hour.

Giving Tempel a wide berth, she crossed the cell and set her hand in Vyroth's. Heat sank into her palm, warming her chilled fingertips. Vyroth murmured in approval, and with a gentle tug, drew her close. She bumped into his side. He tucked her in, wrapping his arm around her.

A tingle swept along her spine.

Nicole exhaled in relief.

"Good to meet you, Niki," Tempel said, dipping his chin.

A respectful greeting. A flicker of warmth in his eyes. Fast and fleeting, but Nicole swore she saw it. Not knowing how to respond, Nicole took a chance and nodded back. "Tempel."

"Time tae go, lass." Kissing the top of her head, Vyroth glanced at his new buddy. "Can you dig us out?"

"Sure, but..."

Vyroth's mouth left her hair. "What?"

"We going for stealth?"

"If possible."

"Then digging's our last resort."

"Too noisy?"

"That—and the structures aboveground might collapse."

"I'm on board with the idea," she said, wanting to lay waste to Montgomery's castle. She didn't care that it was an historical landmark built in the fifteenth century. She wanted the whole place burned to the ground. "Bury them all."

Tempel huffed. "Blood thirsty."

"One of her better qualities," Vyroth said, grinning at her.

"You won't think so when I direct it at you."

Vyroth chuckled and, grabbing her hand, pulled her toward the door. "Niki—how many guards in the house?"

"Castle. It's a castle," she whispered, realizing something. Her heart began to hurt. She gripped Vyroth's hand harder. She couldn't believe it. How could she have forgotten? "And we can't destroy it. Not yet."

"Why?" Tempel asked.

She looked over her shoulder at him. "There are other women being held up there."

Vyroth growled. "Against their will?"

"I think so."

"How many?" Stopping on the lip of the cell, he looked into the corridor. One way, then the other before pulling her over the threshold. He tugged her in his wake, moving from fast walk to jog. "Did you meet any?"

"Two, I think," she said, holding his hand, running

behind him. "I wasn't allowed to mingle, but I saw them in the breakfast room once."

"Bastards," Tempel said behind her.

"You don't know the half of it," she whispered, memories jabbing at her. Every time she fought Montgomery. Each time she lost. Her satisfaction at learning how to deprive him of what he wanted in the end.

"Darlin'," Tempel murmured. "I've spent the better part of three months imprisoned here. I know exactly what's going on."

"How?"

"Vibrations. The earth speaks to me."

She blinked. "Speaks to you?"

"Earth dragon, Niki. Our ways are mysterious."

"Terrific," she said, sarcasm out in full force. "Something else to worry about."

Vyroth snorted.

Tempel grumbled something obscene.

She didn't catch it all. Just as well. Knowing what the huge guy jogging in her wake thought wasn't a priority. She wanted to forget about the pain for a while. Wipe it all clean. Concentrate on the necessary next steps. Worry about everything else later. If only wishing made it true. But as Vyroth led her through the labyrinth, navigating narrow corridors and across wide intersections, Nicole allowed hope to bloom.

Maybe today was her day.

Maybe her luck was finally changing.

At home in Savannah, fortune had blessed her. Her dad loved her. Her sister rocked. Her on-line salvage hunter store had started to grow. Business at the scrapyard was good. She had no cause for complaint. And yet, she'd felt an odd pull her entire life. As though she was stuck in suspended animation. Busy and happy on the outside. Standing still and screaming on the inside. Just waiting for a switch to be flipped and—

"Stop right there!" The shout came from the other end of the corridor. "Don't move a muscle!"

Shock jolted through her.

Nicole turned to look. Three guards stood at the opposite end of the hall.

A siren started to shriek. Cacophonic sound slammed off slimy stonewalls.

"Fuck," Tempel said.

"Niki—behind me," Vyroth growled. "Get behind me."

Nicole didn't hesitate.

Heart thumping, she moved, shifting behind him. Smartest thing to do. Only made sense. Vyroth understood his own kind, and she, her own limitations. And getting in between bad guys bent on destruction and good ones determined to protect her didn't seem like the best idea.

9

―――――

Hemmed in by the narrow corridor, Vyroth stared down the guards at the opposite end. The alarm shrieked. Violence hung in the air, shimmering in the space around him. Widening his stance, he raised his fists, making the males hesitate as he tried to decide—attack or double back toward the intersection serving as hub for multiple passageways.

He needed to find another way out.

A little-known exit to slip out without encountering any more guards.

Outside the odds with the alarm tripped, but still a possibility.

Most prisons had several entrances and exits— some well used, other completely forgotten. Montgomery's underground maze was no different. Vyroth sensed the pathways. Could smell the fresh air. Acknowledged the tingle as day folded into evening. Wraith-like tendrils grazed his skin as breezes snaked down dank corridors from multiple directions, kicking up the smell of must, bringing a new kind of chill. One that invaded his veins and settled in his bones.

Aggression kicked up. Magic rose to greet it. His

dragon half uncoiled, begging to be set free. Vyroth reigned in the compulsion and reasserted control. Much as he wanted to, he couldn't allow his beast out to play.

Not yet.

He needed more space to maneuver—to let his freak fly and his beast roar. An open, starlit sky would do. Though, he'd settle for a high ceiling if push came to shove.

Baring his teeth, he snarled at the males standing frozen fifty yards away. As a unit, the trio shuffled backwards. Gaze riveted on the enemy, Vyroth flexed his hands and unleashed his magic. Heat zipped beneath his skin. His eyes started to glow. Violet and electric blue combined, washing across stone, crawling over the floor and walls. High voltage crackling in his palms, he conjured his lightning. Electricity arched, webbing between his fingertips.

The lead guard's eyes widened.

"Shit, he's juiced!" he yelled. "Lightning—get back! Go back!"

Boots soles scrambling on slick granite, the warriors reversed course. The leader dipped low and swung around. The rear guards caught sight of Vyroth. Both sucked in horrified breaths. The pair turned to flee. Panic made them clumsy. Terror made them trip. One male slammed into the next, taking both down. The lead guard careened into his comrades. The trio banged into the side walls, ping-ponging into each other.

Vyroth scowled.

It almost wasn't fair to kill the trio. The idiots were like helpless puppies. Clumsy. Clueless. Nothing but easy targets, incapable of matching him, never mind—

"What're you waiting for, man?" Tempel growled behind him. "Fry'em!"

Focused riveted on the inept triad, Vyroth amplified his energy. Tempel was right. He couldn't let the males live. Three less to fight later equaled a lighter load. Better odds. Sufficient deterrent too, for any others who thought to follow. Leaving piles of dragon ash in his wake always served to slow the enemy.

Mayhap.

If his luck held.

The retreating males might be the first to die, but wouldn't be the last. With the alarm ringing—and a high-energy female missing—more warriors would arrive soon.

Montgomery wouldn't let it lie. The bastard might not care about him, but he'd stop at nothing to retrieve Nicole.

To be expected. HE females were incredibly rare.

Females as powerful as Nicole were like endangered species—rarely seen and in short supply. Dragonkind males searched their whole life in the hopes of finding (seeing, touching, belonging to) one. For most, those hopes and prayers went unanswered. His, however, had been answered the second Nicole entered his prison cell.

Watching the trio fumble, Vyroth raised his hands. Lightning zigzagged, snapping off stone walls. He wove the streams together, forming a blazing grid. Electricity raked across the ceiling and floor, expanding across the breath of the corridor. He held it a second, listening to the enemy curse, then let the devastating pulse go.

Heat blasted down the corridor.

The lightning grid sizzled over stone, gouging granite walls.

Stone dust exploded from the grooves. The scent of scorched rock infused the air as Vyroth spun toward the other end of the corridor. No sense watching the carnage. He knew what would happen when the pulse caught up with the males.

Nicole grabbed hold of his shirt.

Her gaze collided with his.

He held eye contact a second, then picked her up. Her feet left the floor. He heard her breath hiss in as his arms came around her. He didn't reassure her. He didn't stop. Ramping into a run, Vyroth cradled her against him and snarled at Tempel.

"Dig!" His order rippled beneath the shriek of electricity against stone.

Already standing in the diamond-shaped intersection, Tempel smiled, no humor, all aggression. "Excellent idea."

Webbed lightning reached the guards.

Screams echoed in the passageway.

The acrid smell of burning flesh struck.

Dragon ash exploded up the corridor, dusting the air, coating him and Nicole. Covered in ash, Tempel set his palms against the wall. His green-rimmed eyes began to glow. Earth dragon magic bit like jagged steel teeth, eating into stone.

Solid rock gave way.

Compact earth crumbled.

Wrist deep in rock and dirt, Tempel walked forward. A hole opened in the wall, then widened into a tunnel. Floor to ceiling, side to side symmetrical propositions. Smooth edges. A perfect circle heading into the depths of the earth beneath the castle.

With one last look down the passageway, Vyroth stepped into the breach. The scent of loam and limestone greeted him. Cradled in his arms, Nicole's foot brushed one of the sidewalls. She tucked into a tighter ball. He shifted his hold and swung her around to his back. Her legs and arms came around him. Vyroth wrapped her against him and, carrying her like a backpack, walked backwards, keeping a sharp eye on his rear flank.

Tremors shook the ground underfoot.

Unbothered by the earthquake, Tempel tunneled into the bedrock, magic chewing through fortified foundations, pulverizing boulders, drilling through massive cornerstones on a fast path to freedom.

The alarm continued to blare.

Flakes of dragon ash fell like snow in the corridor.

Lightning webbed between his fingers, Vyroth scanned the entrance to the tunnel. So far, so good. No sign of reinforcements yet. Nothing to do now but hope Tempel found a safe place to surface before more guards showed up and he got caught deep underground with only one way out.

10

P lastered to Vyroth's back, Nicole crossed her feet in front of his stomach and hung on tight. Hands fisted in the front of his shirt. Face tucked against the nape of his neck. Unease at full throttle. And no wonder. With Tempel tunneling through solid rock, weird just kept getting weirder.

Peeking over her shoulder, she watched the earth dragon work.

She'd never seen anything like it.

Dirt and stone disappeared as Tempel excavated. Huge boulders? No problem. He bored holes right through them. Centuries-old foundational stones? No contest. Nothing withstood the force of Tempel's magic. Foot by foot—mile by mile—he moved forward, leaving nothing in his wake. No remanence of once solid bedrock. No dirt or debris. Just a long, smooth-sided tunnel.

Wonder spiked along with incredulity.

She frowned at the side walls. Where was all the debris going?

An interesting question.

One she wanted to ask, but lacked the strength. Fatigue pulled at her. Her muscles burned from fighting to stay balanced on Vyroth's back. An ache bloomed behind her eyes. The sting expanded, raking the sides of her head. Nicole tucked in tighter and, pressing her face into the top of his shoulder, focused on the mission. Namely, holding on as the ground shook and cacophonic drilling intensified.

She squeezed her eyes shut.

Vyroth cupped the back of her head. Searching beneath her braid, he found the nape of her neck. Heat bled from his palm. Nicole sighed as he turned his head and nestled her face into the side of his throat. A soothing wave of... she frowned... *something* hit her. Tingles, sure, but a curl of warm comfort too. The rush rolled over her, smoothing out anxiety, calming the hard slam of her heart one beat at a time.

Her muscles relaxed beneath the flowing stream.

Her legs slipped. One of her feet dropped down. About to lose her perch, she fought her way back up only to slide down a minute later and—

Vyroth's hand dropped away.

He hitched her back into position, securing her on his back.

Doing her best, ankles locked over his stomach, she held on harder. Not a terribly dignified position. Then again, nothing that had happened since she met him qualified as dignified.

Poorly thought-out rescue plan—check.

Scary, uncontrolled dragon guy feeding—double check.

Sloppy piggy-back ride—triple, almost quadruple, check.

If she were the crying kind, Nicole would've let it fly. Too bad pride wouldn't allow it. She'd been through too much, come too far, to give up now.

Hanging on one-handed, she thumped Vyroth on the chest with the other.

Nothing.

No reaction.

Not even a twitch.

She shouted his name, trying to be heard over the roar of Tempel drilling through solid rock. Horrendous noise slammed through the tunnel. Another tremor shook the sidewalls. Her ankle lock failed. As her leg slipped off his hip, she scrambled to hop back up.

She yelled again.

Vyroth turned his head, giving her his profile.

Pressing her mouth to his ear, she said, "You need to put me down. My grip… I keep slipping. I can't—"

He growled at her.

Not a straightforward denial, but she knew he issued one. She felt the force of his *NO* rumble out his back into her chest. Nicole clenched her teeth. Bullheaded. Bossy. Beyond annoying. He ticked off all three boxes, setting fire to her temper. Who did he think he was—the gate keeper? Her lord and master? She might not be fighting fit, but she wasn't a weakling. She could walk. Might even be able to run if things went from bad to worse.

Giving him a squeeze, she conveyed her annoyance.

Ignoring her warning, Vyroth secured his grip on her legs.

Nicole opened her mouth to tell him off and—

Tempel stopped drilling. The thunderous clamour dropped to a low buzz.

"Hold on harder, Niki."

"Put me—"

"Quiet," Tempel said, taking his hands from the

ragged surface of the tunnel end. Dirt coating his arms to the elbows, he turned toward the sidewall. Eyes aglow, he stared at the compacted dirt and, tilting his head, listened to something.

An odd whisper blew through the tunnel.

Reaching out, Tempel set his palm flat against the curved wall. Fingers spread wide, he caressed smooth stone.

His eyes narrowed. A low hum filled the air.

Nicole opened her mouth to ask what he was doing.

Reaching back, Vyroth pressed his finger to her lips.

Absorbing the soft touch, she froze. Her gaze flew to his face.

"Wait," he murmured, hand gentle on her mouth, his gaze riveted on Tempel.

She nodded.

He brushed her bottom lip with his fingertip. Once. Twice. A third time, treating her to excruciating tenderness as the backs of his knuckles left her lips, but didn't stop. Featherlight, he stroked over her cheekbone. Heat swirled down her spine. Captivated by his gentleness, she turned into his touch. With a murmur, he slid his hand into her hair. Wrapping his fingers into the dark strands, he pressed her temple to his.

"This way," Tempel said. "Almost through."

Changing course, Tempel burrowed into the side of tunnel. Decibel levels spiked. Tremors rocked the underground shaft. Stone dust flew as he abandoned one direction and dug in another.

Smart decision?

No way of knowing. Although, his declaration of 'almost through' encouraged her.

But as seconds ticked into minutes, Nicole couldn't be sure. It was taking too long. Montgomery had no doubt been informed. He'd become more than angry. Her escape would send him into a murderous rage. He'd warned her more than once. Made vicious threats. Swore he would never let her go and...

She believed him.

He was too hard-headed—selfish, proud, brutal—to admit defeat.

And as Tempel continued digging, fear grabbed hold. So many questions. Too many unknowns. What if Vyroth's plan failed? What if Montgomery tracked their underground route from the air? He might already be lying in wait, determined to take her back. He might—

Clang! Pop! Bang!

Nicole flinched.

Her head snapped around. Her attention landed on Tempel. Her breath caught. Finally. Thank God—*finally*. He'd punched through into an empty space. Now, he stood in the center of the tunnel he'd dug, bathed in soft light coming from whatever stood opposite him.

Tempel glanced over his shoulder. "We're here."

Vyroth jogged toward the end of the trail. "Where's here?"

"Stuttgart train station." Jumping from the edge, Tempel disappeared into the void. "Underground depot."

"Germany?" she asked his disembodied voice.

"Exactly right, darlin'. Not far from Black Forest,"

"Shite," Vyroth muttered. "See any humans?"

"Storage only. No one around." She heard the crunch across gravel as Tempel walked away from the mouth of the tunnel. "Move it, you two. I need to refill the hole before anyone follows."

Fill the hole?

Nicole glanced behind her. Holding her breath, she listened. The faint sound of footfalls tapped down the tunnel. "Vyroth, put me down or jump. Someone's following us."

"Calm, *Tazleiah*," he said, voice full of reassurance. "The further they are along the tunnel, the better."

Her hand tightened in his shirt. "Why?"

"Cuz I'm going to bury the assholes alive," Tempel said, sounding happy about the prospect.

Swinging her around, Vyroth adjusted her ride from piggy-back to piggy-front and, before she could protest the new position, jumped down. Chilly air went from dusty to fresh. She jolted as his feet slammed into the ground.

Mismatched blue and violet eyes met hers.

Her breath caught.

His gaze drifted to her mouth. "Not yet."

"What?" she whispered back, matching his tone.

"Want your mouth, lass, but now's not the time," he said, rubbing the side of his nose along the side of hers. "When I kiss you the first time, I'll want your full attention."

Her mind tripped over itself. *Kiss her? Her full attention?* Was he insane? She wanted out of the Dragonkind world. Not to wade deeper into it with a gorgeous-eyed guy intent on eroding her foundations and tempting her soul.

From an inch away, she frowned at him. "There'll be no kis—"

"Donnae make promises you cannae keep, Niki." Stroking her back, he settled his hands on her hips. "Okay tae walk?"

"Yeah."

"Hop off, then."

Pretending disgruntlement, more intrigued by his promise of kisses than she wanted to admit, Nicole let him go. As her feet touched the ground, she got her first look at the depot. High ceilings. Concrete walls. Multiple train tracks crisscrossing the cavernous space. Faded numbers painted at the end of each track, and a bunch of ancient railway cars. Best of all —a large station platform thick with cobwebs, eerie echoes, and a well-worn staircase leading out.

"Stand back," Tempel said, standing in front of the open tunnel.

Grabbing her hand, Vyroth retreated, towing her away from his friend. She hopscotched the tracks, following him toward the rail platform, but glanced behind her when the noise started and—

Wicked.

Very cool.

Having an earth dragon around was a definite asset.

Without missing a beat, Tempel conjured all the loam and rock from wherever he'd stored it. Dirt and dust fogged the air. He raised his hands and, like a conductor of an orchestra, directed the streaming earth, funneling it into the tunnel, blasting it back toward the prison.

The hole filled in seconds.

Ramming his hands forward, Tempel shoved, compacting the debris tight.

"I get it," she murmured, dragging her attention from Tempel.

"What, lass?"

"Why you wanted him with us."

"Earth dragons are good tae have around." His

eyes sparked with humor, then hardened into something else.

Conviction, maybe. Pain, for sure. A healthy dose of rage, too. What he felt wasn't difficult to read.

Without thinking, Nicole reached out, set her palm on his chest, and stroked a circle over his heart. It wasn't much. A fleeting touch—there, then gone—but for some reason, she wanted to soothe him. To do for him what he'd done more than once for her.

"Couldn't leave him there, *Tazleiah*. No male deserves what we got in there."

"No one does, Vyroth," she said, thinking about the other women.

"I'll go back," he murmured, picking her thoughts out of thin air. "After I see you safe, I'll go back and get them out—promise."

"You go back, so am I."

"Not a chance."

"They won't trust you, Vyroth. They won't—"

"Done!" Tempel yelled, sprinting across the tracks. "If you two're done making googly-eyes at each other, we need to go."

Vyroth's lips twitched.

Nicole glared at Tempel as he raced past, heading for the railway platform.

Tugging her along, Vyroth ran in his wake.

Nicole scrambled behind the pair, taking the stairs two at a time, eyes glued to the top of the next flight, and prayed for clear sailing. Dragonkind guards might not be chasing her, but that didn't mean Montgomery wasn't ahead, biding his time for a chance to kill her companions and drag her back.

11

Snow-covered peaks jabbed at the night sky as Montgomery flew toward Black Forest. Winter winds bit, whistling over his horns, battering his wings, cranking taut muscles tighter. To be expected. The rocky spine of snowbound Alps wasn't for the faint of heart. Nasty updrafts clashed with his trajectory, determined to push him off course.

His scales rattled in the rush.

Bitter chill dusted him with snow.

His night vision sparked.

A grid of the ground rose in his mind's eye. Using landmarks, Montgomery charted his course and banked into a tight turn. Twin peaks, wind-rush blowing ice off of jagged tips, rose on his right side. Dodging between the lethal spears, he fired up his sonar. Magic blanketed the terrain, rushing down range, along sheer cliff faces into the canyons nestled between.

He rechecked the grid.

Not far now.

Twenty, maybe thirty miles, until he reached the forest edge and home. Blinded by lashing snow, accustomed to navigating winter conditions, he flew straight through the storm. No time to waste. The faster he arrived at Morag Castle, the better.

Cresting the last peak, Montgomery dove over the craggy top toward the valley below. Shale rolled in his wake, clattering down the mountain side. Wind gusts died down. Massive snow-capped peaks gave way to smaller, green-topped mountains. With a flip, Montgomery spiraled across the vale.

Ancient woodland bowed in the face of his speed. Pine needles flew as hundred-year-old evergreens bent in half and snapped back into position. Black Forest howled in protest. He didn't slow. The whiplash didn't concern him. Neither did the broken branches he left in his wake.

Not now.

Not with the moon high in the sky.

Not after the message he'd received from home.

He bared his fangs at the snaking river below. Freaking Vyroth. He knew the male would be trouble the instant he set eyes on him. Too strong willed. Too proud. Far too smart for anyone's good, never mind his own. No matter what he threw at the Scot, he proved unbreakable, possessing the kind of strength Montgomery had rarely, if ever, seen.

Even ravished by hunger, Vyroth remained intractable.

Montgomery growled in disgust. His fault. The entire mess was his fault. He never should've taken the contract. No—strike that. He never should've taken Grizgunn's call in the first place. The whole thing counted as a huge mistake.

The hunt.

The capture.

The imprisonment of a member of the Scottish pack.

Drawing the Scottish commander's notice wasn't a good idea. Ever. Montgomery knew it then, knew it now too. Tangling with Cyprus meant death. At least in the end. The brutality of Vyroth's twin was legendary. Rumors swirled, preceding Cyprus everywhere he went. He might not have met the male, but he'd heard of him. Knew about his warriors too. Vicious. Lethal. Merciless. Words used to describe the dragon pack no one wanted to cross, but...

The money had been too good to pass up.

Clenching his teeth, Montgomery swallowed a curse. Stupid and greedy. He hadn't stuck to the plan. He'd gotten stars in his eyes. Seen dollar signs in his bank account and imagined the ways he would use it.

First priority—providing for his new warriors.

Second on the list—fixing up the castle he now called home.

All to achieve one end—build a pack of his own. A strong one. The kind he never had, but wanted so desperately he dreamed of the day the Archguard acknowledged what the idiots should've known all along —his blood wasn't tainted. He wasn't a gutter rat, but a worthy male deserving of inclusion inside elevated Dragonkind circles.

Prestige.

Honor.

Strong standing with the high counsel and the powerful packs supporting it. Maybe even a seat at the table if he played his cards right.

The contract with Grizgunn, however, threatened everything.

Two months. *Two fucking months*, and Vyroth still sat inside his prison cell. No payment. No word from Grizgunn. Nothing but static from the male who'd commissioned the Scot's capture.

He'd known for weeks he needed to decide about Vyroth... one way or the other. Kill the Scot? Let him go? Angling his wings, Montgomery turned east. He probably should've done it—turned Vyroth to dragon ash and tied off a bad situation. But hope was a tricky bastard, whispering in his ear, telling him it might work out and Grizgunn would pay.

More fool him.

Especially after what happened tonight.

Mind churning, Montgomery set up his approach. Rising from a cliff, Morag towered above the fast-running river, pale façade glowing above a swathe of dark forest. Water frothed around the cliff base before diving into crooked falls. Mist billowed up, fogging the air, wetting rock and the stone bridge arching from one riverbank to the other, from the main castle to the warrior barracks.

Well built. Tested by time. A fixed point to call home. A place to return at the end of each night. A dream come true for a male deprived of hearth and home most of his life.

Widening his wings, Montgomery put on the brakes. He dipped beneath the bridge, then rose hard, swinging around the base of his home. Lit by magic-fueled globes, the courtyard came into view. Spiraling up, he folded his wings. Gravity yanked him out of the sky. His paws slammed into cobblestones. Stone dust burst into a cloud around him, rolling across open space, scrambling toward the front entrance.

The double doors flew open.

Warsaw crossed the threshold. Gaze full of fury, his first-in-command scanned the sky behind him. His eyes narrowed an instant before he fired up mind-speak. *"What the fuck?"*

"What the fuck what?"

"Jesus, Monty," Warsaw said, snarling at him. *"You're flying alone... a-fucking-gain."*

"Few can withstand my venom, Warsaw. And no one can sneak up on me."

Unable to dispute the claim, his friend scowled at him. *"I don't care how strong your magic is, you can't fly solo anymore. It isn't safe. We talked about this, made rules, instated pack protocols. You agreed to all of'em, so no more—"*

"I left Severn and Seagraves to the hunt. Didn't want to pull'em off the scent," he said, trying to placate the male. He didn't need—or want—the lecture. Though...

Much as it annoyed him, Warsaw was right.

Flying solo wasn't smart. No matter how strong, a venomous dragon still required back-up from time to time. No predicting when that might be so... time to lead by example. He didn't want his warriors hunting alone. Which meant, as pack commander, neither could he.

Curling his spiked tail around his front paws, Montgomery sighed. Aerosolized venom rose from his nostrils. *"I'll take more warriors with me next time."*

"Me. You don't go anywhere without me from now on," Warsaw said, drilling him with an unhappy look. *"The others still in Zurich?"*

Montgomery nodded.

"New leads?"

"Couple of good ones." Flexing razor-sharp claws, Montgomery shifted into human form. Magic whispered through his veins. He absorbed the hum and conjured his clothes. Jeans. Long-sleeved tee. Combat boots and leather jacket—his venomous half's uniform of choice. Rolling his shoulders, he dropped mind-speak. "After weeks of nothing, I didn't want

them going cold. Or the asshole going to ground. The male's proving tricky."

"Theives often do," Warsaw said, jogging down the steps. "We encountered a couple of assholes here tonight as well."

"Vyroth, I know about. Who else?"

"Tempel."

"Shit."

"Yeah. We're fucked if we don't get him back, Montgomery."

No kidding. Tempel out of lockdown amounted to a serious problem.

Rodin, head of the Archguard, paid well to ensure the earth dragon stayed under wraps. Why? Montgomery didn't know, nor did he care. Money hit his account every month, no need to ask questions. But if Rodin learned Tempel was no longer under lock and key, shit would do more than hit the fan. A death squad would be sent out... and not just for Tempel.

Rodin didn't tolerate mistakes. Or suffer fools. He cut ties and cleaned up messes without hesitation or remorse.

"How the hell did it happen, Warsaw?" Unease twisted in his gut. "We had both locked down tight."

Skirting his best friend, he headed for the front doors. He ramped into a run, taking the steps three at a time. His feet hit the landing. Montgomery unleashed his magic. Massive double doors slammed inward, opening wide as he crossed the threshold.

The smell of smoke and pine sap hit him. Ignoring the décor, he jogged down another set of steps and, entering the great room, wound his way around ancient furniture. Fire in the hearth hissed, snapping as he made for the main hallway. Two right turns, and he reached the blistered, fire-blackened door guarding the mouth of a spiral staircase.

Unlocking triple deadbolts with his mind, he cranked the doors wide. As he started down the stairs toward the dungeon, hair fell into his face. Raking the white-blonde strands back, he secured it with a tie and looked over his shoulder.

Right on his heels, his first in command met his gaze.

"Start talking."

"Vyroth found a way out of his cell." Footfalls banging against stone treads, Warsaw shook his head. "Far as we can tell, he sprang Tempel."

"They dig out?"

"Tunneled straight through bedrock."

"How many dead?"

"Five." Cracking his knuckles, Warsaw listed the fallen males.

Montgomery clenched his teeth. Five of his warriors *gone*. The youngest of his pack, the least experienced, each one having gone through *first shift* less than six months ago.

"Someone had to let Vyroth out, Warsaw."

No other explanation. The prison cell he'd built for the Scot exploited a lightning dragon's weaknesses. Salt water had been part of it, but keeping him underfed—barely breathing—factored in too. The weaker his captives, the easier to handle, so... yeah. No way Vyroth escaped without help.

Reaching the last step, Montgomery traversed an intersection. "You find the turncoat?"

"Well..."

Moving at a fast clip, he glanced over his shoulder. "Who?"

"The female."

"Nicole?"

Warsaw nodded. "There are markings on the lock into her cell. She picked it."

Already peaked, his temper went from simmer to a hard boil.

Montgomery ground his back molars together. Clever, clever female. Another pain in the ass, but also... gorgeous in her relentless resistance. Tenacity coupled with fierce intelligence. Just a couple of the many things he loved about Nicole. Brainy, beautiful, full of life-giving energy. Everything about her called to him. Was she spirited? Yes. Was she stubborn? Absolutely. Was she everything he wanted in a female? Without a doubt. The instant he saw her in Prague he'd known she belonged to him.

"Where is she now?"

"Gone."

"Fucking Scot."

Bane of his existence. He never should've targeted Vyroth. Or trusted Grizgunn to keep his word. If the Dane had done as he promised, Vyroth would've been long gone by now. Out of sight, out of mind. Good fucking riddance.

Now, instead of a healthy bank account, Montgomery had problems. Big ones—the kind no smart male wanted in his ledger. Had Nicole not been involved, he would've said to hell with it. Called Rodin. Returned the money. Allowed Vyroth to slither back to Scotland. But with his female gone—stolen from the very home he planned to make with her—he refused to turn a blind eye.

Turning left, he moved toward Nicole's cell. Insult added to injury. A trespass of the worst kind. Vyroth had taken his female, touching what didn't belong to him. The offense couldn't go unpunished. Honor demanded he retaliate. Primal need dictated he tear Vyroth limb from limb. Intellect won the day, allowing him to form a plan on the fly.

He would do what he did best—hunt the assholes down.

Nicole would be retrieved.

Tempel would be recaptured.

Vyroth would never be seen or heard from again.

He didn't care how it happened, or in what order. Just as long as the Scot died, and Nicole ended up back under his control. Problems with Cyprus and the Scottish pack be damned.

12

Leaving dank, musty air behind, Vyroth crested the last step. Five flights up from the underground train depot, not another set of stairs in sight. He scanned the wide landing. High ceiling with a bunch of different colored pipes. Tiled floor scuffed in spots, stained in others. Three bright blue doors to his right. A cinderblock wall with peeling paint running along the left.

No one milling around.

Not surprising. The signs on the walls stated—Authorized Personnel Only.

Tempel had done well. The train depot had been the perfect place to break through. The space allowed Vyroth to acclimatize. After two months of confinement, he needed a minute. A second or two to get his bearings and calibrate his sonar.

Fresh air enlivened him.

Long-denied dragon senses fired.

Information scored through his mind. Sound and scent narrowed into sharp focus. He heard the clamor of footsteps beyond the last door. The chatter of voices joined by a man's voice calling over a PA system. The hum as trains came and went on electrified tracks.

Close.

He was so close. Almost there. Access to open skies less than a mile away.

His hand flexed around Nicole's.

Breathing hard from running, she squeezed back. "Okay?"

"French fries and hamburgers, lass." Vyroth breathed deep. Warm air tainted by the scent of fried food filled his lungs. He closed his eyes. Bloody hell, that smelled good. "Nothing like it."

"So we're close?"

"Very," Tempel murmured, pressing his hand to the wall between two doors. "Main terminal through here. A hop, skip, and jump away from the front doors."

A furrow between her brows, Nicole stared at Tempel.

The male raised a brow. "What?"

"Your accent. I'm trying to place it." Biting the inside of her lip, she studied him. "Are you American?"

Tempel shrugged.

Nicole kept at him. "Boston?"

"Close, but not quite. Born and raised up north... in Salem."

"Salem... makes sense. You seem pretty witchy to me."

Rolling his eyes, Tempel raised his middle finger and flipped Nicole off.

Vyroth's mouth curved. "You two done bonding?"

"One of my countrymen," Nicole said, hitching a thumb in Tempel's direction. "Pretty cool."

Tempel glared at her, then shifted his bad temper in Vyroth's direction. "You gonna keep your female in check?"

"Hey!" Full of affront, she pointed at Tempel. "No need to—"

"Too much power, Vyroth. High-energy. Rare. Never seen anyone like her before and... you know—you know the danger," Tempel said, voice full of warning. "He feed from you, darlin'?"

Catching his drift, Nicole paled. "None of your business."

"That's a yes. Sorry, Niki, but..." Eyes full of regret, Tempel shook his head. "No way Montgomery lets her go, man. He's fed from her, he can track her. Which means he'll track us unless you lock down her connection to the Meridian."

"W-what?" Looking from Tempel to him, Nicole pressed closer. "What does that mean?"

"No time to alter her signal," he said, ignoring her question, focused on the male making a very good point. Energy regression, however, wasn't the solution. Not right now. Not until he got Nicole somewhere safe.

Energy regression was serious business. Never to be taken lightly. Or done against a female's will.

If she allowed it, he'd need days to shift her energy signal—the pulse she sent out into the world—not hours. Once a Dragonkind male fed from a female, he could sense her across vast distances. The idea Montgomery possessed the ability to track Nicole enraged him, threatening his control.

Clenching his teeth, Vyroth locked down his reaction. Fury wouldn't serve him. He couldn't change the past, or take away his mate's pain. All he could do now was make sure Montgomery never got near her again.

"So muffle it." Hand gripping the doorknob, Tempel gave him a level look. "Mess with the signal."

"I'm already doing that," he said, annoyed with his friend. Did Tempel really think he hadn't started muting Nicole's energy the second he touched her? "But we need distance too. The farther away we get, the harder it'll be for him to trace her energy."

"Oh my God," Nicole whispered, hand trembling in his.

"Darlin'."

"Oh my God!"

"Niki, calm. Stay calm," he said, trying to soothe her.

"Is it true? Is what Tempel said true?" Fingers curled in his jacket, she yanked on his arm. Frightened light brown eyes met his. "Can Montgomery track me? Can he really—"

"Shh, *Tazleiah*." Reacting to her fear, he dropped her hand and cupped her face.

Stroking over her cheekbones with the pads of his thumbs, he dipped his head. No thought, all need, his mouth brushed hers. Pleasure burned through him, opening a fissure inside him, making him ache from the inside out.

Unable to stop, he kissed her again... and again.

Softly.

Sweetly.

With an aim to soothe, not arouse. But as his mouth settled more firmly on hers, something miraculous happened. She responded, tipping her chin, offering her mouth, blooming beneath his touch. The more she relaxed, the more he took, introducing her to his taste, getting a contact high from hers.

"Twill be all right, lass."

"But if he can track me, we're screwed. We're... I can't go back, Vyroth." Tears in her eyes, she fisted her hands in his shirt and released a shaky breath. "I can't."

"You willnae. I willnae allow it," he murmured

against the corner of her mouth. "Trust me, baby. I'll keep you safe."

Kissing her one more time, Vyroth drew her deeper into his arms. She burrowed in, holding on tight, trusting him to lead, strong enough to follow. Relief streamed through him. Gratefulness followed. Beautiful Nicole. Such a strong female. Smart. Proud. Capable of doing for herself, and yet, she leaned on him, giving him what he needed to keep her safe.

"You need to be touching me at all times, Niki. Skin-to-skin, got it?"

"To muffle the signal?"

"Aye."

"Okay."

Mouth pressed to her temple, he glanced at Tempel. "How well do you know this area?"

Tempel shrugged. "Probably better than you."

"You have a plan?"

"Got better than that. Gotta safe house."

"Where?"

"North. In Cologne."

"North's good," he said, unable to believe his luck. The further north he flew, the closer he came to Scotland—to his brothers-in-arms and back up. Only one drawback—the miles to travel before the sun rose and UV rays fried them both. "Can we make it before daybreak?"

"Yeah, just."

"When we get out there—head on a swivel. Stay cloaked. Stay close. Fast in flight."

Tempel nodded. "Link in first."

Good idea. A much-needed tactical advantage.

Mind-meld would allow him to communicate and coordinate with Tempel from miles away. Members of the same pack linked in all the time, entering each other's mental space without effort. With one noticeable caveat—the magical bond couldn't be forced. Both males must not only agree, but forge the connection.

Magic spiraled onto the landing as Tempel initiated contact.

He knocked on Vyroth's cerebral front door.

Vyroth hesitated. Forging a mental link with anyone other than his packmates felt alien. Uncomfortable. Risky. Ill-advised. He didn't know Tempel well. Then again, the earth dragon could say the same of him.

Patient in the face of his unease, Tempel met his gaze and waited.

Vyroth stared back. A beat passed before he decided to trust the male. Reaching out with his mind, he grabbed hold. The link solidified as his mind aligned with Tempel's.

"Fuck." Tempel blinked. "Lightning."

"*Earth*," he said, using mind-speak, feeling the powerful flow of his friend's magic.

"*Time to fly the coop.*"

"*Go.*"

With a nod, Tempel cranked the knob, yanked the door open, and stepped over the threshold. Treating himself to another kiss, Vyroth nipped Nicole's bottom lip, then grabbed her hand, and followed his friend into a corridor, praying he made it into open air before Montgomery and his goons showed up.

13

Holding tight to Vyroth's hand, Nicole exited the stairwell behind him. She caught a quick snapshot of the hub before the crowd blocked her sightline. Seemed ordinary. Nothing special on the train station front.

The unusual part was the number of people.

Multiple platforms teemed with all shapes and sizes. Short. Tall. Thick and thin. Some passengers disembarked from arriving trains. Others stood waiting impatiently to climb onto scheduled-to-depart ones. Scent and sound collected beneath high canopies rising over multiple trains, protecting more than one platform. The smell of grease and exhaust clashed with the scent of roasted peanuts. Rapid footfalls rapped across ceramic tile, blending with a voice calling over a PA system.

The crush grew thicker.

Vyroth shoved through the throng, joining the flow of human traffic. Lacing her fingers through his, she fisted her other in his jacket sleeve. Crowds weren't her favorite thing. Never had been, but the last month had made her aversion worse. Close quarters reminded her of confinement and her short-lived experience inside a prison cell.

Her stomach churned.

Inhaling through her nose, Nicole exhaled out her mouth. Memories rose to haunt her. Brandishing a mental shield, she beat each one back, tucking the hurt away, burying painful echoes deep in the back of her mind. She didn't want to think about it. Or turn and face the fear. And self-reflection? She huffed. No need for that. Later would be soon enough to deal with what happened. Right now, she needed to concentrate.

Staying on Vyroth's heels meant everything.

Everything.

Freedom. Safety. Comfort.

The idea should've bothered her. Somehow, it didn't. She might not know him well, but *not knowing* him didn't matter. Nicole knew what she needed to about him.

He was solid. He was safe. He was on her side.

Getting to know him in the ordinary way involved the kind of superficialness she refused to entertain. She wasn't on a first date. She and Vyroth were way past the usual questions. All the little things people asked on dates, scratching at the surface, diving into the minutia of another's life. Trusting Vyroth entailed something different. She sensed the connection. Could feel the bond growing, forging deeper, increasing its influence with each passing second.

Another thing that should freak her out.

She embraced it instead.

He wasn't a normal guy. She'd never been what anyone called an ordinary girl. In a weird way, she made sense with him. And, despite all the strange dragon stuff, he belonged with her.

Which made her either crazy or stupid.

Her sister would agree. Full stop. No need for discussion, but...

Nicole peeked at Vyroth from the corner of her eye. She studied him, trying to figure what drew her, why he'd become so important in such a short amount of time. Seconds ticked past as she moved through the terminal with him. After a full minute, she gave up trying to understand.

Her reaction to him was unquantifiable.

Odd and unexplainable.

And yet, kind of nice.

As the thought streamed through her head, she realized something even more startling. She wasn't afraid of him. At all. He didn't energize her unease. Vyroth soothed her instead, steamrolling over anxiety, smoothing out her rough spots, leaving serenity in its wake.

The tension she carried drained away.

Movements fluid, she followed as he cut a swathe through the crowd, maneuvering around benches and steel pillars, up staircases, passed slowpokes with eyes glued to cellphones. Strides even. Pace steady. Eyes scanning above the crowd. Direction set, arrival at the final destination he imagined assured.

Taking a sharp turn, he sliced through traffic against the grain. A man bumped into her. With a low snarl, Vyroth shoved him away. The guy careened toward a garbage can. The crowd scattered, splitting open, providing a clear avenue in front of him.

Tempel snorted. "Temper, temper."

Teeth still bared, Vyroth glared at him. Eyes shimmering with unleashed aggression, his gaze dipped to her. "All right?"

"I'm good, but can we get out of here?"

In the lead now, Tempel strode toward an escalator.

A woman gave him a dirty look, then scowled at Vyroth.

Smothering a laugh, Nicole speed-walked to keep up. The second he reached the escalator, Vyroth drew her forward. He nudged her onto the moving treads and stepped on behind her. Sandwiched between two Dragonkind warriors, Nicole looked around. Low sloping ceiling. Bad artwork made worse by graffiti. People giving the lethal duo hemming her in covert glances and very wide berths.

The sound of running trains died down.

The smell of fast food drifted down the stairs.

"Main terminal up ahead." Taking the stairs three at a time, Tempel sprinted toward the top of the rise.

"Go, lass."

Understanding what he wanted, Nicole ran up the remaining steps. At the top, she veered left, tracking Tempel across the main terminal. Restaurants, fast food joints, and shops located along one side. Kiosks sat in the middle, beneath arched windows reaching toward the vaulted ceiling. Doors exiting onto the street in every direction.

Skirting a row of benches, Tempel sidestepped a man on a cellphone.

Nicole watched the guy end the call and slide the phone into his back pocket.

Coming even with him, she veered into his lane. Her shoulder caught the side of his arm. The man jerked back in surprise. His roller bag listed to one side.

"Sorry, sorry," she muttered and, as he righted his suitcase, lifted the phone from his jeans. Pocketing it, she walked away, pace quick, heart hammering, afraid he'd notice he was now one cellphone light of a load.

A couple of strides behind her, Vyroth closed the distance. As his arm wrapped around her, he dipped his head and set his mouth to her ear. "Wee pickpocket. Very smooth, lass."

His voice chased a pleasant shiver down her spine. "Dad taught me."

Retreating enough to catch her eyes, he kept her walking and raised a brow. "Your Da?"

She shrugged. "Unconventional childhood."

"Much more interesting than mine."

"Doubtful." Warmed by his approval, she smiled at him. Good to know she could impress him with her unusual skill set. And to know she still possessed her abilities. It had been a while since she'd grifted... or worked a mark. Her dad might be respectable now, but he hadn't always been what society considered an upstanding citizen.

Raising two daughters as a single dad straightened him out. Mostly. But not before she and her sister learned a few interesting lessons.

"I need to call home." Pulling the phone from her pocket, she tilted it in his direction. "Can you unlock it?"

He nodded and flicked his fingers.

Static electricity buzzed over her hand. The Samsung came to life. The numbered keypad flashed, then stayed, on screen.

"Thanks."

"Make it quick, Niki. You've got until we get outside. The second I shift, the signal will cut out."

Focused on the phone, she let him direct her and dialed. Nothing happened. Clutching it tighter, she glanced at the screen, searching for the problem, praying the call connected. She placed it back against her ear.

A soft click.

The sound of a ringing. Once, twice, a third time, then—

"Hello?"

"Cate?"

"Niki?"

At the sound of her sister's voice, tears blurred her vision. "Yeah, Catie. It's me."

"Oh my God. Oh my God," her sister whispered. "Where are you? Are you alright? You've been missing for—"

"Cate, listen for a sec." Her voice cracked. A tear rolled over her bottom lashes, making her lean harder into Vyroth. "I can't talk long."

"What the hell is going on?"

Vyroth gave her a squeeze of encouragement.

Missing her sister so much it hurt, Nicole soldiered on. "I'll explain everything—I promise, but not right now. I don't have a lot of time. I just wanted to let you know I'm okay. Tell Dad—"

"Are you safe?"

"Yes. Yes, I'm safe," she said, looking up at Vyroth. "Safer than I've been in a really long time."

Setting his mouth against her temple, he murmured against her skin.

"Thank God, thank God." Cate's voice broke as the line crackled. "Dad and I have been going crazy. We filed a missing person's report with—"

"Catie—I have to go," she said, reaching a large bank of glass doors. "I'll call again when I can."

"Niki?"

"Yeah?"

"Come home. Please, come home."

"Quick as I can." A lie. Bold as brass and twice as ugly. *Quick* wasn't within her power to promise. Not with Montgomery nipping at her heels and Vyroth determined to keep her. Freedom now didn't mean a swift return home later. Intuition warned unyoking from Dragonkind would take considerable effort. A long, slow untangling. "Love you, Cate."

"Love you too."

She didn't say goodbye.

Her heart refused to let her. It wanted to hold on, keep the connection, comfort her sister while she reassured herself.

Breathing hard, struggling to control her tears, Nicole stared at the off button. A death grip on the phone, she closed her eyes. God. She couldn't do it. Couldn't disconnect unless Cate hung up first. Born eleven months apart, inseparable growing up, she and her sister had always been best friends.

Seemed wrong to let her go. Wrong to—

"Give it to me, lass."

She hesitated.

He murmured in understanding and, patient in the face of her pain, waited for her to angle the phone in his direction. Holding her gaze, he tapped on the screen, disconnecting the call. Her chest hollowed out. An agonized sound escaped her.

"You'll talk tae her again, aye?"

"Promise?"

"Aye, lass. You've my word."

As she wiped tears from her cheeks, he moved her toward a bank of doors. One swung open without him touching it. He guided her through into night air and the rising hum of traffic.

Waiting on the sidewalk, Tempel took one look at her and frowned at Vyroth. "What the fuck?"

"She called home," Vyroth said, removing his arm from her shoulders, recapturing her hand.

"And you let her?"

"I needed to talk to my sister."

"You have a sister?" Expression arrested, Tempel stared at her, no doubt contemplating a swift flight across the Atlantic.

"Touch her, and I'll kill you."

Tempel grinned, the picture of a too-charming guy bent on disobeying.

Her eyes narrowed in warning.

Vyroth pried the phone from her hand and tossed it into the nearest garbage can.

"Hey! I need that."

"I'll get you another." Towing her behind him, he stepped off the curb into the busy street. Traffic screeched to a stop. Drivers yelled, voices muffled, making rude hand gestures from behind the safety of windshields. Vyroth ignored the angry hue and cry and, weaving between stopped cars, headed for a parking lot across the street. "Eventually."

"Reassuring," she said, sarcasm escaping her control. "Thank you."

Amusement sparked in his eyes.

Resisting the urge to maim him, she treated him to a withering stare. Not that it worked. Her attempt to blast him with attitude bounced right off him. Vyroth was immune, too busy scoping out the parking lot, seeking out dark corners away from prying eyes and street cameras.

Nicole knew what he was doing.

Tonight wasn't her first rodeo.

She'd witnessed what Dragonkind could do in Prague the night Montgomery kidnapped her. He and his crew didn't wait for privacy. The assholes had shifted in the middle of the street. No fear of discovery. Zero worry about being seen in dragon form. Killing all chances for her to escape.

"Vyroth?"

"Aye?"

"Warn me before you—"

Tiny streaks of lightning exploded around her.

Cold air evaporated.

Vyroth released her hand as he transformed, shifting from man to dragon. Warm scales brushed against her. Hot breath rushed over the top of her head. A voice pushed past her mental guards, entering her head, making her temples tingle.

"Niki—look at me."

Arms hugging her chest, eyes squeezed shut, Nicole shook her head.

"I'm not like him, baby."

"I know, but... it's just..."

"Look at me, Niki. Really see me."

Nails biting into her palms, Nicole inhaled deep and exhaled slow. She filled her lungs again. In. Out. Repeat. She could do this—find her courage, be brave enough to face what she believed she never wanted to experience again.

Courage, flower petal.

Her father's words drifted through her head. *Flower petal.* She hadn't thought about his nickname for her as a little girl in years. Somehow, though, the sound of his imagined voice gave her strength. What she needed to shove the bad down deep and bring up the good.

Vyroth wanted to protect, not hurt her.

Opening her eyes, Nicole tipped her head back.

Her gaze collided with mismatched dragon eyes. One iris electric blue, the other pale, shimmering violet. She looked closer. Vyroth stared back, then rolled his massive shoulders, inviting her to look. Breaking eye contact, she ran her eyes over him, taking stock, absorbing the sight of him in dragon form.

Lord. Everything about him was beautiful. The dark blue, silver-flecked scales. The webbed wings pressed against his sides. Even the vicious horns rising from his head to join clusters of large and small spikes knifing along his spine, stopping at his bladed tail, looked cool. Her attention landed on his paws. Huge by any standards. Razor-sharp claws. Hooked tips. One hundred percent lethal.

She released a pent-up breath. "Holy crap."

"Just me, lass. Same male, different form," he murmured inside her mind.

"Can I..." Her fingers curled, betraying her thoughts. She wanted to touch him. In Prague, she'd been on solid ground one second, in the air the next. She hadn't gotten a good look at Montgomery and hadn't wanted to touch. All her focus had been on getting away. "Is it okay to touch you?"

"Another time." Sharp claws clicked as he opened his talons. "Climb in."

She stared at the proffered paw.

Not very subtle. Hard for her not to get the message.

With a simple gesture, he asked for complete trust. He wanted her to set aside prejudice and to go all in with him. To trust him and forget the hurt she suffered at the hands of his kind. A bold strategy all things considered. One she appreciated. As far as tactics went, it was a good one.

Holding his gaze, she pursed her lips. All right, then. Ball in her corner. Time to decide—be brave or allow fear to rule.

Pride nudged her.

Setting her knee on the side of his paw, Nicole climbed in. Long talons closed around her. Heat bubbled up, creating a warm cocoon as he unfolded his wings, surged upward and...

Lift off.

She heard his wings beat. Felt scales rasp against her skin. Listened to her heart tattoo the inside of her chest as Vyroth angled into a turn. Closing her eyes, she curled up inside his paw and settled in for the flight. Nothing else to do. She'd made her decision. Now, she must live with the consequences—no matter what the night brought or how bad things got.

A strong tailwind worked in his favor, pushing him north toward Cologne. Using powerful strokes, he throttled up his wing speed, staying on Tempel's tail. Dark brown scales speckled gold and green glinted ahead of him. A little to his left.

Thank fuck for the moonglow.

What little light broke through thick cloud cover allowed him to see the earth dragon in full flight. Impressive. A little startling. Tempel was huge. Much bigger than most warriors in dragon form. Vyroth wasn't a lightweight by any standards, but Tempel tipped the scales with a larger than normal wingspan. Rings of spiraling spikes rode the length of his spine. Massive paws with tri-pronged claws tipping each talon were a revelation.

Triple the claws.

Three times the impact.

All the better to dig—and kill—with, he guessed.

Dipping left, Vyroth scanned the dark canopy of forest below. Nothing but trees and narrow winding roads below. The occasional blink of lights from houses nestled on the mountainside in the woods.

Pretty enough, but what he wanted was the sight of tall buildings and the glow thrown by city lights.

Cologne couldn't be far now.

No more than an hour away.

Rotating into a flip, Vyroth leveled out on Tempel's wing tip. A northeasterly gusted over the treetops. Giant evergreens swayed. Cold air blasted over his horns. His scales rattled in the wind rift, buffeting the protective shield he held around Nicole.

She swayed on his back, bumping against the bubble.

Afraid of losing her seat, she scrambled to grab better handholds. Small hands grasped against blunted spikes.

Stabilizing her, he murmured, pushing into her mind, talking to her, encouraging her to relax. He needed her to trust him. To flow with the flight instead of fighting to stay on.

A big ask under the circumstances.

Even though he would never let her fall, he understood her nervousness. Her first flight with a dragon hadn't been pleasant. The second he left the ground, her mind took flight, rambling into dangerous corners, feeding him details. No matter how hard she battled, she couldn't suppress the memories.

With each passing minute, more collected inside her mind. Little things. Major events. Experiences she tried so hard, but kept failing, to forget.

Now, she relived the night Montgomery took her.

And Vyroth saw everything.

The brutality. The savagery of her fight. Her denial of Montgomery followed by her expulsion from the main lair. The long, slow, dark walk into the dungeon.

His throat went tight.

Goddess keep her. She was a beautiful wee warrior. So fierce she broke his heart.

Nicole had strapped on the few weapons she possessed and gone into battle to protect herself. Gave up luxury, fancy gifts, and delicious food. Fought Montgomery every step of the way, choosing honor over comfort and personal gain.

Vyroth bared his fangs. Bloody hell, he was proud of her. Blessed to call her his own, but...

The bastard.

The fucking bastard.

Montgomery needed to be put down. Fast. Sooner than that if possible.

Males who hurt females didn't deserve to live. Forcing an energy connection, taking without a female's consent, was a violation of the worst sort. Humans called it rape. Dragonkind treated it as a death sentence. No male worthy of being called Dragonkind crossed that line without being forced to face the consequences.

Vyroth wanted to be the one to do it.

To bring Montgomery to ground.

To take him apart inch by agonizing inch.

To play in the bastard's blood before he ripped his head off.

He toyed with the idea a moment, then let it go. Losing control now wouldn't serve him—or Nicole. Control, cunning, a solid strategy was the best way forward. Montgomery wasn't stupid. The male knew how to hunt and kill. The trick would be luring the bastard into a kill box without him knowing Vyroth put him there. Something to look forward to and—

Nicole's hands scrambled against his scales.

She blew out a shaky breath.

He continued to talk to her, using magic to disturb

the jagged line of her memories. Seconds ticked into minutes before she grabbed the mental lifeline he offered, letting him all the way in.

"*Good, lass,*" he whispered, pushing further into her mind.

"*I'm so tired. I don't want to think about it anymore.*"

"*I know, baby. Hold on, stay connected... I'll see you through.*"

He waited for her to answer.

She replied without words, folding forward, lying down in the space between his spikes. Her cheek pressed to his scales, she nestled in, flowing with his course corrections, instead of fighting the flight. Her surrender gave him hope. She wasn't relaxed. Not exactly, more like too exhausted to care.

Already rundown, needing a decent meal, she'd reached the end of her rope, lacking the strength to stay upright. Not that she was in any danger of falling off. He held her secure. Magical tethers kept her in the saddle. The warm pocket of air he controlled kept her from feeling the arctic-fed winds.

A good thing.

The best, given her condition.

She might be a strong female, but being kidnapped had taken its toll.

Monitoring her vital signs, he linked in and took her temperature. Warm enough. Heartrate a little high. Energy levels acceptable, but lagging. Not dipping into the danger zone so far. That, however, would change if he didn't reach the safe house soon. His female needed hours of sleep in a soft bed under thick blankets.

Tempel explained the layout.

Three floors of ancient house located in the city center. Lots of bedrooms, plenty of space, a state-of-the-art kitchen. A powerful protection spell sur-rounded the property, making the brownstone not only impenetrable, but also invisible to males who didn't belong to the Belarus pack. The perfect set up, not only to ensure Nicole's comfort, but to contact Cyprus and mobilize his brothers-in-arms.

Needing a timeline, Vyroth fired up mind-speak. *"Tempel."*

"Yeah?"

"How close are we?"

"Three hundred and fifty miles out."

Vyroth clenched his teeth. Not good news. Further away than he expected. He'd hoped the city was closer. Around the bend. Over the next rise. Three hundred plus miles meant staying airborne longer than he wanted. Flying at the maximum speed, if the wind held steady, Cologne would appear on the horizon just before dawn.

"Anything closer?"

"Nothing but forest for miles. Nowhere safe to land, given who's on our tails. I'd rather turn and fight—"

"Nay. I cannae risk—"

"Niki. I know, man. Were I you, I wouldn't risk her ei-ther," Tempel said, sounding resigned and aggrieved at once. *"How's she doing?"*

"Moving from dog-tired into completely exhausted. She needs a warm bed... good food."

"Forty-five minutes—an hour, tops. Keep her warm and well-fed until then."

Vyroth grunted. An hour. Hell. He hadn't realized Germany covered so much ground. Though, he should've known. If he'd done his homework before leaving Scotland, distance and geography wouldn't be a problem. Usually, when he left home, he researched the countries he crossed. Knew every detail, right down to how many warriors called different areas home.

Three months ago, he'd left in a hurry without doing the usual due diligence.

He hadn't intended to stay in Prague long. A quick trip to gather intel—an in and out mission. Obtain the information he needed to locate his cousin, then get the hell out. Even so, he never should've flown into Archguard territory unprepared.

Lesson learned.

Again. For the second time in his life.

His uncle (commander of the Scottish pack before Cyprus) had warned of trouble years ago, pulling his support, refusing to kowtow to the males on the high counsel. Greed fueled the ruling families of Dragonkind. Lust for power—political maneuvering to possess more—topped the ever-lengthening list of rapacity.

The things he'd seen and heard in Prague, the complete disregard of what best served Dragonkind as a whole, shouldn't have shocked him. Somehow, though, it had. He expected more from the leaders of his kind. The pampered aristocrats never seemed to do the right thing. Nothing new. The power struggle was real, old as time. The Archguard wanted to stay in power while craving more. Unscrupulousness and ruthless agency in politics was par for the course— two sides of the same corrupt coin. Depravity, how- ever, belonged in another category... was something else entirely.

Something dangerous.

Something avoidable.

Something that would split Dragonkind in half, and eventually start a civil war.

Rodin, leader of the Archguard, remained oblivious. The male wanted what he wanted—to hell with anyone else. A reckless attitude given the current political climate.

Vyroth huffed. His nostrils flared. Electricity sparked in the darkness as he angled his wings, changing his trajectory to stay with Tempel.

Reckless.

Understatement of the century.

Rodin wasn't just playing with fire. He fanned the flames. Corrupt, power hungry, selfish and short-sighted, the male exhibited all the traits of a megalomaniac. He believed himself untouchable. A false assumption. One time would rip wide open, disabusing Rodin of the notion.

No one was unreachable.

No one was un-gettable.

And no one, no matter how powerful, was immune to a dagger to the heart.

Sooner or later, pack leaders all over the world would react. Some would back Rodin, others would mount strong opposition against him. In fact, the divide was already happening. From what he knew, the Nightfury commander in Seattle had already entered the game, making strong moves to dismantle the Archguard and send Rodin packing.

An interesting turn of events.

Everyone wanted out from underneath Rodin's toxic thumb. His pack included. Forget about the twice-yearly tithes deposited in Archguard accounts. Eliminate the ancient customs that no longer made sense. Admit times had changed (Dragonkind along with it), and new traditions needed to be—

A tingle swept over his horns.

His sonar pinged.

"Fuck," Tempel growled. *"You feel that?"*

"*Aye—company.*" Fine-tuning his radar, Vyroth sent out feelers. His magic spiraled across the night sky, skimmed the forest, and... aye. Right there. Bold as brass, breaking through the three-mile marker, tracking Nicole, trailing him and Tempel into northern Germany. "*Montgomery.*"

"*Stupid to warn us they're coming.*"

"*Maybe the bastard just doesn't care.*"

"*Arrogant.*"

"*Soon tae be dead.*"

Tempel laughed.

The rough sound whispered through Vyroth's head, pricking his senses. "*Half an hour away now—give or take?*"

"*About right. The plan?*"

"*Secure Nicole inside the safe house. Set the trap, reel the bastards in and—*"

"*Kill'em all.*"

"*How many you got on radar?*"

"*I count four, three miles out.*"

"*Two more are in the weeds. Hanging back, trying to stay out of the count.*"

"*You sense them?*"

"*Aye.*" He sensed everything, picking up details most Dragonkind males never registered. As a lightning dragon, his skillset was varied—command of electricity in all forms, the neuro-toxic, electro-static pulse he exhaled, the ability to unearth details about enemy males from miles away. Information like age, magical strength and type of exhale. His was a rare skill most of his kind never witnessed.

"*The usual variety?*"

"*One venomous dragon, one acid, three fire-breathers. The sixth exhales Scald.*"

"Excellent. A challenge," Tempel said. *"Nothing I like better."*

"Then you're good."

"Man, you have no idea."

Vyroth grinned at his friend's temerity. Nothing he enjoyed more than a vicious male looking forward to a fight. But first things first. He must reach Cologne and the safe house before Montgomery's pack reached him.

Nicole needed a safe place well away from the battle.

He wanted to be unencumbered when he met the enemy. Able to maneuver without worrying about her when his claws cut through scales and dragon blood began to flow.

15

A deep murmur stroked her awake. The voice tapped against her temples, gently adamant, supremely annoying. Mind tangled in woolly snarl, Nicole struggled to acclimate. A curl of sensation ghosted through her. She floated in the stream, tracking the prickle across her skin.

A warm caress down her spine.

A soft tug at her temples.

The gentle slide of an addictive ghosting touch.

Nicole sighed. So nice. Just what she needed. She wanted to stay here—wherever here ended up being—forever. The lovely stroke came again, nudging the edge of her mind. The soothing baritone followed, pulling her from the stream, lifting her through layers of sleep.

"No." With the side of her face mashed against something, the word came out wrong. Muffled. Butchered. Croaked. Nicole didn't care. She wanted to stay exactly where she lay—cocooned in warmth, cradled by relaxation. "Go. Away."

A chuckle chased the prickle through her mind. *"Niki, my love."*

The endearment spun through her. Parts of her gone untouched for years woke up. Nicole drifted in the fullness of it. No one other than her family had ever loved her. Not really. Not truly. Oh, she'd heard it a time or two—a couple of old boyfriends (both trying to get into her pants), but she discounted it—then and now.

"*Tazleiah—come on, baby.*"

She hummed. *Baby* was good. *My love* sounded better. "What?"

"*Time to wake up.*"

"Too soon," she said, resisting the gentle urging.

"*Hate tae do it, lass. I know you need sleep, but we're here,*" he said, coaxing her, separating her from slumber one word at a time. "*I need tae explain what's happening.*"

"Happening?" Her eyes drifted open. Nothing but blur. She closed them again.

"*I need you tae ride with Tempel a wee while.*"

The news jolted through her.

Nicole went from half asleep to fully awake in point five seconds. Flat.

Her mind rocketed to the on position. Where she lay registered. She jerked upright. Her cheek left warm scales. The first thing she saw—a dark blue dragon head with hooked horns. The second thing that came into view—the sharp rise of buildings and the glow of urban lights.

Cologne.

One of the most beautiful places in Germany.

She knew the city. Had visited on her quest to find lost objects. Things she could fix up and repurpose— all the rare gems most people thought of as garbage. Throwaways from long forgotten decades. Vintage pieces she collected from all over the world and sold online.

She'd found some beautiful pieces in Cologne.

Right before she left for Prague.

Using his spikes as handholds, she shifted on his back. Her gaze trailed over the skyline. Lit up like a beacon, Cologne Cathedral rose above the cityscape, twin spires reaching for the stars. Smaller buildings sat in its shadow, colorful facades and steep-angled roofs clustered like petitioners around a priest.

Banking into a turn, Vyroth executed a rapid descent. Hanging on tight, she watched him come in low, then level out. His bladed tail lashed treetops as he flew over the concrete bank of the Rhine river. Water rippled, chasing him across the surface as wings spread wide, he blasted over the bridge and blazed into the city center.

Eyes skimming building tops, she tried to get her bearings. To remember the names of crisscrossing streets and neighborhoods. "What's the plan?"

"When I say so, Tempel's going tae pick you up."

"Vyroth," she whispered, disliking the plan.

"I know I promised, lass, but Tempel's the only one who can open the safehouse." Angling his wings, he sliced between two buildings, then swung around a spire. *"I donnae belong tae the Belarus pack. The house willnae open for me."*

"But..." she trailed off, not understanding. He wasn't making sense. "You're coming to the safehouse with us."

"I need tae watch our backs. Cover him while he lets you in."

Alarm tripped through the back off her brain. *Watch their backs? Cover him?* None of it sounded good.

Her grip on him tightened. "What the hell's going on?"

He hesitated, answering her question with silence.

She read his intent. Knew exactly what he was doing—shielding her. Protecting her from whatever held his attention. Maybe he believed she couldn't handle the truth. Maybe he feared frightening her. Maybe his need to keep her safe—from *everything*—trumped his usual affinity for honesty.

Nicole understood the dilemma. Be honest, risk freaking her out. But she hadn't climbed into his paw for nothing. Somewhere along the way, she'd started to trust him. *Really trust him,* so—no. Vyroth keeping secrets—deciding what was best for her, how much to tell her, what she could handle—wouldn't fly.

Not with her. Not right now.

"I'm stronger than you think I am. Tell me."

"Fuck," he said, more growl than actual word. *"It's going tae happen fast, Niki. Tempel will take you. He'll set down hard, open the door and point you toward it. Donnae hesitate, lass. Get inside and do it fast."*

"Why?"

He sighed. *"There's a pack on our tails."*

"Montgomery?"

"Aye."

Her stomach clenched. "He's following me?"

"Only way he'd be able tae track us."

Nicole closed her eyes, blocking out the city. Heaven help her. Talk about a bad outcome. Nothing had gone right since the night she arrived in Prague. So many wrong decisions. Too much of it her fault. Had she just stayed in her hotel room instead of visiting Prague's outdoor market at night, none of it would've happened. She'd be scrounging through scrapyards, antique shops, and estate sales, looking for tarnished things to turn into treasure.

Her kidnapping would never have happened.

Montgomery wouldn't be chasing her.

She would never have met Vyroth.

The last thought jarred her. Nicole shook her head. She didn't like the idea of not meeting Vyroth. Her mind rebelled at the idea. Something about him called to her. The fact she'd known him less than a day didn't matter. She felt the connection and understood the rarity. Most women looked their whole lives for a man like Vyroth—strong, protective, genuine in his care of her. Which meant...

She couldn't regret any of it. Not the kidnapping. Not her experience inside Montgomery's lair. None of the pain. All of it had led her straight to him.

"Vyroth?"

"Aye?"

"You're going to kill him, right?"

"Guaranteed, lass."

She nodded.

He skimmed an ancient apartment complex, then banked and circled back. *"Ready?"*

For Tempel to pick her up? No, she wasn't ready. But what could she do? Arguing about it wouldn't change the circumstances. Resisting the plan would only waste time, so... no help for it. Time to buck up and do the necessary thing to avoid an ugly one.

"Go."

The second the word left her mouth, a giant dragon paw plucked her off Vyroth's back. She yelped as she left her seat. The bubble around her burst. Cold air hit her. Tri-clawed talons closed around her. She peered through the gap between the dragon's fingers.

Dark eyes rimmed with green flashed as Tempel folded his wings and dropped out of the sky.

Massive paws slammed into the ground.

Momentum carried her up. Gravity dragged her back down, smacking her into Tempel's palm. Air left her lungs. With a wheeze, she rolled face up. Giving her no time, Tempel set her down. Her shoe soles collided with a stone surface.

Nicole looked down at her feet, up at Tempel, then around the courtyard.

Open to the street, ancient-looking brick buildings rose on the other three sides. Old-growth trees stood sentry inside the large, rectangular courtyard. Multiple paths, interrupted by winterized flowerbeds, led to more doors than she could count in the second Tempel gave her.

"Move it, Niki," he said, snarling at her.

"Where?" Remembering Vyroth's warning, she swung to face Tempel. Ignoring his fangs and all the jagged brown scales, she asked, "What address? Where am I going?"

Heat blasted through the courtyard.

A wall on the far side of the courtyard went wavy. An instant later, a large archway, wide black doors tucked in the alcove, materialized in the solid brick wall.

Nicole lunged toward the entrance. Her shoes slid on slick cobblestones. She kept going and, taking the most direct route, sprinted between trees, through flowerbeds, kicking over clay pots, her eyes on the double doors.

Her focus narrowed on the fancy gold knocker.

Almost there, she reached for the handle.

A second before she made contact, the black lacquered panel cracked open.

Thunder bloomed, shaking the buildings. Lightning forked overhead, cracking over the city. Claws scraping over stone, Tempel leapt skyward.

Flapping wings blew violent wind gusts across the courtyard. Trees creaked as branches thrashed. The storm surge shoved her forward.

Slamming into the door, she pushed it wider, then turned and yelled, "Be careful! Tell him to be careful!"

Tempel didn't answer.

No surprise.

He had bigger fish to fry. Namely reaching Vyroth before Montgomery and his crew reached him.

The thought gave her pangs. She might be new to the nuances of Dragonkind, but instinct warned a fight between dragon warriors would be vicious. Nasty. Bloody. Ruthless. Without rules or mercy. A game at which Vyroth and Tempel both excelled, given the brutality inside the prison corridor.

Nicole released a shaky breath, replaying the escape in her mind. The screaming. The awful smell of burning flesh. Dragon ash falling like rain.

Like rain.

The fact Vyroth had gotten her out alive should've reassured her. He was strong. He knew how to fight. He understood his own kind. Nothing Montgomery tried would surprise him.

A fortifying thought.

Too bad it didn't console her.

Feet rooted to the floor in the foyer, surrounded by expensive wallpaper, listening to eerie echoes inside an empty house, Nicole couldn't shake the feeling something terrible was about to happen. Worry crept in, amplifying unease, making her imagination run wild. Worst case scenarios popped into her head.

Anything could happen. No one was invincible. Vyroth included.

Which left her wishing she'd told him herself, instead of yelling it at Tempel. She wanted him to be careful. She needed him to come back. Otherwise, all she'd be was an odd girl standing in a strange house wishing for a second chance with a man she barely knew, and common sense insisted she shouldn't want.

16

Violent storm clouds gathering above him, Vyroth rocketed out of downtown. Slithering like a serpent, the Rhine snaked under bridges, sliding past barges tied to concrete piers. Shoreline nothing but a blur, he blasted over the river. Thunder boomed over Cologne. Whipped into rough chop, water frothed in his wake. Houses along the bank shook. Window glass rattled. Lights blinked on behind bedroom curtains.

Electricity crackled, whipping off the tip of his tail.

Another deafening boom.

Cloaked in magic, hidden from human eyes, Vyroth fine-tuned his sonar, ignoring the lightshow overhead. Nothing new. He produced electrical charge everywhere he went. Tonight, though, the powerful current felt different. Usually, he controlled it better, but with emotion running high, his magic amplified, giving his beast more leeway.

He should lock it down. Now. Before his dragon half got the better of him.

Leaning into the tempest, Vyroth let it roll, loving the sound, the sight, the power as thunderclouds growled and barbed bolts lit up the sky. Cologne wouldn't be the same. Humans would talk of the storm for weeks, along with electrical surges and sudden power outages.

Parts of the human power grid were already down, opening up black spaces, making the cityscape look like an unfinished puzzle, gaping holes in the image.

Another good reason to pull the plug.

Leaving people without heat on a cold winter night wasn't his MO.

Vyroth waffled a moment, then reined in his dragon half. The beast bared its teeth. He growled back and re-tasked the energy, directing it toward his objective. Magic flowed in front of him, devouring artic air, throwing down grid, mapping the city topography and the forest beyond. Thin threads blanketed the area, giving him the lay of the land. Gathering the intel like bread crumbs, Vyroth banked around a pair of high-rises and headed south.

His sonar pinged.

A blip appeared on his radar.

He recalibrated and—five miles away. Fantastic. The night was about go from good to fun. Montgomery was close, flying straight toward him. Right into his teeth.

Dipping low, he moved from scale-rattling speed to fast glide, skimming building tops, his gaze rapt on the horizon. Slowing down just about killed him. He wanted to fly full tilt into the enemy pack. Arrive like a wrecking ball. Do serious damage. Break bones and see dragon blood flow as he tore Montgomery apart.

Not the smartest play.

Much as it pained him, he needed the bastard alive.

At least, for a little while.

The male possessed answers he needed—not only

to understand the past two months, but also to make a full report to his brothers-in-arms. The rationale behind his imprisonment might not matter to his vicious half—his dragon didn't care about semantics. The beast wanted to kill... the end. Most of the time, Vyroth was on board. Problem was, the reason he'd disappeared for months would matter to Cyprus.

His twin liked information. More intel—concise data—was nirvana when it came to his blood brother. The Scottish commander didn't fool around. Cyprus believed in being prepared. Knowledge equaled power, the kind that fed good decision-making.

Which meant, he couldn't rip Montgomery apart.

Not yet.

He must, at the very least, attempt to find out why he'd been targeted and caged. Otherwise, Cyprus would lose his mind and aim a nasty amount of attitude in Vyroth's direction.

Velocity set to maximum, Vyroth left the suburbs. Back over thick forest, he tracked the pack of six. He scanned the skyscape. A small town to the east. The Rhine to the west. Not much in between. No sign of the enemy yet.

His sonar buzzed. His eyes narrowed. Four miles out, a minute or two away from breaking through the three-mile marker.

Blasting over a tiny lake, he fired up mind-speak. *"Tempel?"*

"Here." Slicing between lightning bolts, Tempel dove out of thunderclouds. Wings spread wide, he flipped up and over. Storm flash strobed over his dark scales, making the green and yellow flecks on his dragon skin glow. *"What'da we got?"*

"Three and a half miles out," Vyroth said as his friend settled on his right wingtip. *"Niki?"*

"Safely behind closed doors."

"Any trouble?"

"Nope. She's fast for a female. Didn't hesitate. Asked me to tell you to be careful."

"Christ."

"You gonna listen?"

"Unlikely."

Tempel snorted in amusement.

Vyroth grinned at the sound, then got serious again. *"Though, I should at least try tae be smart."*

"What'da mean?"

"Goes against everything in me, but..."

Tempel sighed, picking up his train of thought. *"You don't want the asshole killed."*

"Not yet," he said, tone full of regret, but adamant.

Montgomery and his pack would die—badly, violently, while screaming—eventually. For more than just caging him. The bastard had committed one of Dragonkind's cardinal sins. An unforgivable crime. He'd hurt Nicole. Taken his female off the street. Held her against her will. Touched her without her consent.

His dragon half frothed at the thought.

Vyroth bared his fangs, imagining what he would do to the male. Slice him to ribbons. Skin him alive. Watch him dissolve into a pile of dragon ash. The fact he needed to curb his base instinct, the one insisting he protect his mate, enraged him. Delayed gratification didn't suit him. He was a strike first, never ask questions, kind of male. And now, with Nicole safe and primal instinct marauding, the urge to avenge her slid under his skin, right into his heart.

As her mate, he owned the right to extract retribution by law. To seek justice on her behalf. To be the one to right the wrong and help make her whole again.

"*You want answers,*" Tempel said, frustration in his voice.

"*Aye.*"

"*Fuck, but...*" Flying alongside him, Tempel's green-rimmed eyes glowed with aggression. His lip curled, baring one huge fang. "*I could use some too.*"

"*So—agreed?*"

Tempel growled something obscene.

Vyroth took that as a yes. "*Doesn't mean we cannae turn the screws. He needs tae be breathing tae talk, not whole.*"

"*Finally. An idea I can get behind.*"

Vyroth snorted. As electro-static current crackled overhead, his sonar tightened the net. Six pings sounded inside his head. Two lead dragons came into view. One light blue, the other red. Neither male was Montgomery.

"*Two separate fighting triangles,*" Tempel said. "*You going left or right?*"

He assessed the pack. His gaze snagged on Montgomery. Vibrant green scales. Black horns and claws. Poisonous daggers tipping his spiked tail. A venomous dragon in full flight, toxic to the bloody core.

Fury rolled through him.

Prey in his sights, Vyroth flexed his razor-sharp claws. "*Left.*"

"*Keep it tight, man. Remember the plan.*"

Excellent advice.

One problem.

As he swung wide, setting up the attack, his dragon half took over. The plan ceased to matter. All he saw was Montgomery. All he felt was murderous rage. All he wanted was to right a wrong and avenge his female. To hell with the rest.

17

Coming in hot, Vyroth hit the lead dragon like a freight train. The male snarled and, claws deployed, swung at his head. A quick duck. A fast shift. He dipped under the vicious swipe and, lightning sizzling between his talons, raked his claws down the male's side.

Electricity bit like a buzz saw, cutting through flesh.

Blood splashed up his forearm as the blue dragon spun away, trying to avoid a second strike. No such luck. Locked on his prey, Vyroth hammered him again. His claws sank deep. He yanked, pulling the male sideways through the air, slicing through enemy scales. The male howled and, fighting for his life, whipped around.

Vyroth's hold on him loosened.

His claws ripped free.

He lost his grip.

Not wasting a second, the blue devil whirled into a tight turn. His double-bladed tail swung with him. Scales rattled. Knife-like spikes gleamed in the storm glow as the bastard aimed for his head.

With a growl, Vyroth dodged, rotating into a three-hundred-and-sixty-degree flip. The enemy strike sailed wide. Tucking one wing, keeping the other open, he revolved into a sideways somersault, pivoting in the opposite direction, making the enemy guess. Deception at its best. Strategy put to the test, ensuring the trio surrounding him didn't get a clear shot.

If Montgomery wanted to down him, he needed to do a lot better.

Surrounded by three males, Vyroth banked one way, then the other. Quick bursts of speed. Faster changes in trajectory. A yellow dragon gave chase, staying on his trail. Angling his wings, Vyroth slowed down. He wanted the bastard closer. Almost on his tail. So close, the male never saw it coming.

Vyroth counted off the seconds.

One, two and—

Claws brushed the tip of his tail.

Throwing his head back, Vyroth twisted into a back-flip. White streaks streamed from his wing-tips. The male chasing him squawked in surprise. Landing behind him, he snagged the bastard's tail and wrenched it backwards. Yellow scales cracked. Bones snapped. Brutal sound echoed as lightning flashed overhead

The blue devil circled back around.

Claws buried in the enemy's tail, he spun full circle. At maximum speed, he let the yellow dragon go, throwing him like a shot put. Out of control, wing webbing torn, the male hurtled toward his comrade, impact imminent. He didn't wait to witness the two collide. He was more interested in watching another male plummet out of the sky.

Banking into a turn, Vyroth searched the airspace. His eyes narrowed, he called on his magic. Invisible threads of electrical current rolled across the sky. No ping on his sonar. Zero sign of Montgomery. Not a whisper of movement or sound.

He fine-tuned his radar.

Nothing but Tempel hammering enemy males on the skyscape.

Vyroth frowned. Had Montgomery gone to ground? Had he left his comrades behind? Abandoned his warriors to the ruthless skill of a lightning and earth dragon combo? Seemed unlikely. Montgomery might be depraved, but he wasn't a coward. He had to be here—somewhere. Hanging back. Waiting for an opportunity to strike. Setting up the best sight line to unleash his venomous exhale.

Circling back around, Vyroth made another pass.

Split into two groups, the enemy fought three-by-three. One trio on him, another on Tempel. A solid strategy. He would've done the same in Montgomery's place. Three against one was considered good odds... when dealing with ordinary Dragonkind warriors.

He and Tempel, however, were anything but ordinary.

With his lightning and Tempel's earth, two against six didn't mean much. Especially in close-quarter combat. Fast in flight, skilled in claw-to-claw, Vyroth didn't need to unleash his exhale, but at least he had the option. Fighting six against two in open sky, the enemy couldn't say the same. The instant an enemy male unleashed his exhale, he risked hitting one of his own. Friendly fire wasn't taken lightly by Dragonkind. No warrior wanted to be responsible for downing one of his own.

Movement flickered in his periphery.

Yellow and blue scales flashed.

Vyroth bared his teeth. The duo was back up, airborne despite the injuries he'd inflicted.

Avoiding slashing talons, fangs, and sharp tails, Vyroth rocketed between the two, hammering one male on the fly-by. The yellow dragon's head snapped back. Wing-flapping, the blue devil countered, taking a sharp turn. Diving under swiping claws, Vyroth aimed for the bastard's throat. His knuckles crackled against blue scales. Air exploded from between the blue devil's fangs as he stabbed the yellow dragon with the tip of his bladed tail.

Both males reeled backward.

Vyroth conjured a lightning lasso. Wrapping the ends around his paw, he wielded the double loop like a whip. Electricity cracked. Cold air heated. Sizzling blue current sliced through enemy scales. The duo roared in pain.

Dragging both sideways, Vyroth tightened his grip.

His sonar pinged.

A flash of green scales materialized behind him.

Busy slicing the enemy dragons to ribbons, Vyroth heard the inhale. Bad move. All kinds of stupid. Montgomery should've stay quiet—remained cloaked and lost in the crowd. Instead, he'd gotten greedy, given away his position along with his advantage. Now, Vyroth knew exactly where the bastard was—right where a smart dragon never wanted to be... in a lightning dragon's sights.

Locked onto Montgomery, he released the lasso, leaving electrified barbwire tangled around the undynamic duo. As the pair fell, wings bent at odd angles, he hung in mid-air, making himself a bigger target, and waited for Montgomery to strike.

Three.

Two.

One...

Montgomery exhaled. Venomous green mist shot

from between his fangs. Toxic swill rocketed toward him. Bilious stench devoured fresh air, eating the oxygen, sticking like poison to the back of his throat.

Holding his breath, Vyroth held the line.

A second before it hit him, he folded his wings and dropped like a stone. The toxic cloud shot over his head. Free and clear, he opened up. His webbing caught air. Muscles pulled as he swung around and, fangs bared, went after the depraved male who'd kept him confined for months.

Montgomery sucked in another breath, intent on exhaling again.

Vyroth struck him broadside. Pain rippled over his shoulder. Grappling with the warrior, his claws scraped over green scales. Trying to gain separation, Montgomery threw his horned head back. Unable to avoid the backlash, Vyroth turned his face away. Montgomery's forehead crackled against his temple.

Bone cracked against bone.

His vision blurred for a second.

An instant was all Montgomery needed.

Blood trickled into his eye as Vyroth struggled to hold onto the bastard. Montgomery twisted, elbowing him in the head, gaining separation. Roaring, he pushed off and somersaulted away.

With a snarl, Vyroth chased him, nipping at his tail, trying to sink his claws into flesh. The instant it happened, he'd drag the male from the sky. Fly him straight into the ground and hold him down hard. Trust Tempel to keep the remaining warriors away while he extracted answers from the male responsible for wounding Nicole.

He swiped at Montgomery again.

A burst of orange appeared on the horizon.

Vyroth clenched his teeth. Hellfire. He'd forgotten

the time. The glowing thin line reminded him, peeking over the forest. The sun was coming up, pushing its poison through the darkness, lighting up the eastern sky. He needed to get a hold of Montgomery... fast. Otherwise, he'd lose his opportunity. Daybreak would shut him down—force him to abandon the fight, turn back toward Cologne, avoid the deadly UV rays as the night vanished and the day took hold.

"*Vyroth,*" Tempel snarled through mind-speak. "*We need to bug out.*"

"*One more minute.*"

"*Fuck, man—don't.*"

He heard the words and understood the underlying panic. Tempel was smart. What he said made perfect sense. Dragonkind couldn't survive in daylight. Contact with UV rays caused blindness and eventual death. He and Tempel both needed to head for home, but...

Bloody hell.

He couldn't let the bastard escape. Montgomery needed to answer for his crimes. The male deserved death, not freedom. The bastard wouldn't stop. He'd hurt other females, imprisoned more males. The suffering needed to stop, and he wanted to be the one to ensure it happened.

Firing on all cylinders, speed supersonic, he swiped at Montgomery's tail again. Sharp spikes grazed his palm. He stretched harder. Dagger-like barbs bit. Pain spiraled up his arm as cuts opened between his talons.

In full retreat, Montgomery snapped his tail and broke away. With a roar, he called his warriors to order. The trio fighting Tempel swung wide and circled around, following their commander as he bugged out.

"Vyroth!" Allowing the enemy to retreat, Tempel flew to intersect him. *"Think of Niki."*

Tempel's growl stopped him cold.

Nicole. His female. The one meant and made for him.

Spreading his wings wide, Vyroth put on the brakes.

Tempel was right. He needed to blanket his rage and screw his head on straight. Abandoning Nicole wasn't an option. He refused to leave her alone all day. She wouldn't understand if he didn't make it home. His absence would feed her imagination, make her worry and fear the worst—his death.

"Hell."

"Exactly," Tempel said, flying toward him. *"Have you pulled your head out of your ass?"*

He grunted in answer. She might be new to him, but his female deserved certainty. As much as he could give her. Dragonkind wasn't a timid or peaceful race. Warriors fought and died all the time. But to force her to wonder about his safety when he held the power to reassure her didn't sit well with him.

Probably never would.

Swiping blood off his chin, Vyroth pivoted into an about-face. Struggling to control his fury, he watched the enemy pack skip across the fast lightening sky. Head tipped back, he snarled at the coming dawn. Didn't help his frustration. Made him feel like an idiot, but... so close. *So bloody close.* He'd been a whisper away from grabbing Montgomery and slamming him horns first into the ground.

Almost.

Almost.

Almost.

The word pounded the inside of his temples. Almost wasn't good enough. A few more seconds. Another five minutes, and Montgomery wouldn't be an adversary anymore. He'd have been his toy. Something to play with as he waited for his brothers-in-arms to arrive.

"Goddamn it." Disappointment a bitter pill to swallow, he ripped his gaze from the enemy pack and rejoined Tempel. The sun crept higher in the sky, eating at the gloom, making his scales prickle in warning. *"I had him. I fucking had him."*

"Live to fight another day, brother." Flying off his right wing-tip, Tempel bumped him with the side of his tail. Huge spikes rattled against his interlocked dragon skin. No pain involved. Not even a bruise. Just a love tap, one meant to encourage and console. *"We'll get him."*

"When? It might take months for the bastard to pop his head up again."

"Eventually, man. The asshole needs to work. He can't hide forever."

True. Still... frustrating as hell.

He disliked the idea of *eventually*. Vyroth wanted *now*. But with his female waiting at the safehouse, living to fight another day would need to do—for now.

18

F inishing her tour of the house, Nicole left the third-floor and walked down the back stairs. The one off the front entrance was much grander, almost opulent with a superbly crafted banister, honey-colored wood polished to a high shine. She'd walked up it to explore, sticking her head in bedrooms and bathrooms (even a linen closet or two), making sure the mansion stood empty.

No skeletons in the closets.

Not a soul to be found in any of the rooms.

Nothing but comfortable furniture patinated by time.

Expensive stuff. All in good taste. Hand-crafted by master builders from centuries gone by. If she hadn't guessed already, the elegance of the place would've given it away.

People with money lived here.

Lots of it.

Wide-planked wooden floors gave way to narrow stair treads. Well-worn grooves cupped her soles, cradling her socked feet, as she descended toward the main floor. The house had seen lots of traffic. Been lived in and well-loved for years. Witnessed countless of lives lived.

Old bones. Good vibes.

Hand-carved baseboards and crown moulding stood in relief against plaster walls with fresh coats of paint. Pictures of landscapes and historical battles graced the hallways. Ancient woven rugs lay like lounging soldiers on each landing. She'd seen many on her tour—some big, others small—giving the house a comfortable, well-lived-in feel. Everything about it screamed welcome, sit down and stay awhile.

Lovely, but...

She couldn't get comfortable.

Coming around the last curve, she set her hand on the sloping railing. Smooth wood slipped beneath her palm. She concentrated on the slide, hoping for calm. Worry reared its ugly head instead. The second Tempel dropped her off, low level anxiety had gone to work, buzzing like bees inside her chest. Now, everything felt too tight—her muscles and bones, her mind and heart.

Her imagination spun, conjuring worst case scenarios.

Vyroth hurt.

Vyroth at the mercy of Montgomery and his crew.

Vyroth dead and turning to ash.

Pausing on the last step, Nicole closed her eyes. She didn't want to think about it. Didn't want to believe he might not come back. Her chest tightened at the thought. She deep breathed through it, forcing her lungs out of lockdown. Steady inhale in, long exhale out. Another set. More deep breathing. She needed to settle her mind and deal in facts, not the worst *what ifs.*

Vyroth knew what he was doing.

A man as strong as Vyroth didn't go into battle unprepared. He possessed powerful magic, weapons that made other dragon guys back up in a hurry. She'd seen it firsthand. Had witnessed the fight in the prison hallway. Her brow puckered as she replayed it in her head.

Fight was, perhaps, understating it.

Annihilation, complete and utter devastation, was far more accurate.

The guards hadn't stood a chance once Vyroth unleashed his lightning. He was strong, smart and decisive. He wouldn't take unnecessary risks, which left her wondering why she worried at all. The smart thing to do was swipe the slate clean. Eliminate the status quo from her vocabulary and embrace the truth. She wasn't living in a world she knew anymore. She now inhabited a different one—Dragonkind's. Which meant she needed to start trusting Vyroth.

Really trusting him.

He kept asking her to leave the limitations of her old life behind and enter into a new reality. One no one but Dragonkind—and few humans—lived inside. Here and now, alone in a gorgeous house, shielded by magic, seemed like a good time to rise to the challenge.

Imagining the worst wouldn't get her anywhere.

Denying the truth would bring nothing but heartache.

Trusting Vyroth to keep his word felt a whole lot better.

Blowing out a breath, Nicole exited the stairwell and crossed the back hall into the kitchen. She stopped beneath the arched entrance to get the lay of the land. Huge space serving three purposes—kitchen, dining area, and family room. Her gaze skipped across the open plan. Vaulted ceilings showcasing ornate coffers with tin tiles. The entire back wall windowed with a view to a back garden. Pale grey cabinets, black marble countertops. Stainless appliances, oversized grey-and-white tile floor set in a diagonal pattern. Massive kitchen island with a deep sink and seven low-back chairs tucked under the lip.

Nicole stared at it. The thing had to be fifteen feet long.

A wooden table, golden top scarred by use, sat between it and the family room. She counted sixteen curved-backed chairs, eight down each side. Walking farther into the room, she bypassed the island to run her fingers along the top of a chair. Her attention jumped to the large flat screen over the fireplace. A massive sectional made its home in front of the stone mantel, wood stacked neatly on the grate in the hearth, waiting to be lit.

Designed with comfort in mind, the multipurpose room took up half of the first floor. Didn't seem like Dragonkind guys did anything *small*... or in half measures.

Chewing on her bottom lip, Nicole turned back toward the kitchen.

She needed something to keep her busy. Taking stock of the pantry and fridge should do it. Maybe if she scavenged a bit, she'd come up with ideas for a solid meal. Something the guys would no doubt appreciate when the pair got home.

Worry poked at her again, replacing *when* with *if they made it home.*

Nicole shoved the thought aside. She refused to

entertain any more negativity. Things were burning hot enough without her adding gasoline to the fire.

Flipping cupboards and drawers open and closed, she took stock. Lots in the pantry. Nothing in the fridge but condiments and a container of grated parmesan cheese. Stuffed full, the freezer provided tons of choice—thick steaks for BBQing, all kinds of fish, and a bag of homemade meatballs.

A quick plan formed.

She yanked the meatballs out, closed the freezer drawer and, dumping the bag beside the eight-burner gas stove, headed for the pantry. In minutes, she got set up. Pots on the stove, two burners firing, one with water set to boil, the other with pasta sauce. The meal wasn't fancy. Nicole didn't care. Spaghetti and meatballs were healthy, filling, exactly what Vyroth and Tempel needed after chasing enemy dragons across the sky.

Watching the clock, she stirred the sauce, then pulled the pasta off the stove. Steam billowed as she dumped the noodles into a colander in the sink and—

A door slammed.

Sound reverberated through the house.

A tingle swept over the nape of her neck.

Vyroth.

He was back.

How she knew was anyone's guess. But with knowledge born of certainty, she knew he'd just crossed the threshold.

Heart in her throat, she abandoned the meal and, skirting the island, moved toward the double arched entrance into the family room. The sound of heavy footfalls fell. Air in the house seemed to crinkle, folding in on itself as static electricity entered the kitchen. Nicole drank the spiking energy like water, pulling it in through her pores, using it to quench her thirst.

Intense need rolled through her.

She needed to reach him... now. To do more than see him. She wanted to touch, run her hands over him, make sure he was okay. Nicole didn't question the urge. She allowed it to lead. Upping her pace, she rushed under the archway and—

Got her first look at him. "You're hurt."

"*Tazleiah*, I'm—"

"Bleeding!" she said, her tone accusatory.

"A scratch, lass."

A scratch? She scowled at him. Half his face was covered in blood.

Boots planted in the wide front hall, he raised a brow.

She ignored the annoying challenge and, striding forward, met him beside the round hall table. Pulling him around it, she cupped his jaw. Prickles of awareness ghosted up her arm as she tilted and turned his head. Her focus landed on his wound. Patient in the face of her inspection, he allowed her to prod the diagonal cut slicing from temple to brow with her fingertips.

"Jeez, Vyroth. You could've lost an eye."

"Didnae," he murmured, stating the obvious, wrapping his arm around her.

"What happened?"

"Got clipped."

Focus on the cut, she frowned. "By what—a broadsword?"

He huffed. "Tip of a tail."

"Montgomery?"

"Aye."

"Asshole."

Tempel chuckled.

She turned her frown on him. "And you? Are you alright?"

"Scrapes and bruises. A couple of cracked ribs, nothing a good sleep won't fix."

Nicole sucked in a breath.

"Shite, brother," Vyroth said, shuffling her backward, giving Tempel room to pass. "Should've said something."

"What would it have changed?" Holding his side, Tempel limped beneath the archway into the family room. "With the sun coming up, no choice but to get home."

Vyroth grunted and followed his friend. "Smells good, lass."

"Spaghetti and meatballs," she said, watching Tempel plant a hand on the kitchen island. He swayed. A grimace flashed across his face. Nicole's stomach clenched as he wiped his expression clean. Total tough guy, trying to hide the pain. Knowing he wouldn't like it if she offered help, she wrapped her arm around Vyroth's waist and cleared her throat. "You guys hungry?"

Two growled yeses came back in answer.

Clear enough.

Time to feed her tough guys.

"Sit," she murmured, stopping beside the table. Meeting Vyroth's gaze, she gave him a squeeze. "I'll dish up, then get you cleaned up."

"Medical supplies in the hall bathroom, darlin'."

"I know."

Tempel raised a brow, throwing the scrape on his cheek into sharp relief. "Did some exploring?"

"Had some time."

Still holding his ribs, he nodded.

"Sit down before you fall over, Tempel."

"Gonna grab some grub, then head to my room. Once I sit down, I'm not getting up again."

Vyroth snorted.

Nicole hustled around the island to the china cabinet. Flipping a glass-fronted cupboard open, she brought down three bowls, two large, one small. The work of seconds, she mounded pasta into Tempel's, added sauce, grabbed utensils, and planted it in front of him.

His mouth curved as he looked at the huge helping.

"Enough?"

"It'll do, darlin'. Thanks."

His gratitude warmed her, making her feel less like a victim, more like a contributor... as though she were part of the team. Nodding at him, she left the other bowls empty on the countertop, stacking the smaller one inside the bigger. Perfect fit. Yin and yang in complete harmony, one vessel resting inside the other.

Nicole stared at the coupling a moment. Strange, but it seemed important. Like a message denied finally delivered, a visual reminder that not everything needed to be difficult. Sometimes things just *fit*. No need to question it. Zero reason to fight it. A cause to celebrate instead of flee.

"Lass?"

The gentle inquiry came from right behind her.

She touched the lip of the bigger bowl. "Yeah?"

"You alright?"

Good question.

She wasn't sure. As foolish as it seemed, the bowls

signified something. Something she didn't understand, but knew was real, indelible, and right.

Vyroth cupped the nape of her neck. He dipped his head. His mouth brushed her ear. A pleasant shiver rode along her spine. Drinking in his heat, she let go of her resistance and turned toward her favorite pastime—discovery.

Curiosity was a long-time friend of hers. She liked to tinker, take things apart, put it back together, make it work like new. When something caught her interest, the object of her inquiry held it until she understood everything about it. Unusual for most people, an obsessive pastime for her. And Vyroth? She found him endlessly fascinating. Only natural for her to want to know more about him. His history. His likes and dislikes. All about his family and what it meant to be an identical twin.

A strange reaction given all she'd been through.

A man shouldn't interest her. Not right now. She shouldn't want his hands on her. But as he stroked his thumb along her throat all thoughts of plotting the next move—of figuring out how to hide from Dragonkind while she found a way home—disappeared.

She couldn't deny the attraction. Or quell the ruthless need to know. Like always when faced with something of interest, she banished the idea she shouldn't ask and embraced the one stating she ought to know *everything*.

Forget playing it safe.

Vyroth interested her.

Period.

No need to put a leash on her inquisitive nature.

"Bathroom," she whispered, enjoying his soft caresses.

"What?"

"I'll clean you up first, then we'll eat."

Mouth drifting over the side of her neck, he murmured his assent. "Tempel—you got a phone?"

Pulling out a drawer beside the island chairs, he tossed something at Vyroth. "Calling home?"

Nipping her shoulder, Vyroth caught the cordless phone in mid-air. "Gotta let Cyprus know. We need back-up."

"I'll call in my commander when I get upstairs."

"Sleep well."

"You too, brother." Tempel picked up his bowl. Boots thudded across the floor. A second before he crossed into the back hall, he glanced over his shoulder. "Gotta a feeling, though, I'll get more than you."

"Hopes and dreams, lad. Hopes and dreams."

Tempel laughed.

Setting the phone down on the counter, Vyroth brushed his hands over her shoulders and down her arms, raising goosebumps, making her lean into him. Wicked knowledge burned through her as her spine met his chest. He would be amazing in bed, gentle and thorough. So very *thorough*, leaving none of her un-touched—body, heart, mind and soul. She should take a beat to re-evaluate and find the best way forward.

She didn't.

Didn't hesitate or think twice.

Allowing instinct to lead, she leaned into need and, turning her head, pressed her forehead against his jaw.

Rough whiskers scraped over her cheek.

She sighed. "You're really warm."

"You're very beautiful."

Her lips curved.

Lovely compliment. Simple and straightforward.

Not that he needed to shower her with praise. His

gentleness, the tender way he touched her, the patient way he waited on her, allowing her to decide, set the stage. Informed her mind and tugged at her heart, giving her the courage to continue what he invited her to start. And with Tempel gone, she not only had time and opportunity, but the will to accept what he offered.

19

Taking his hands from Nicole just about killed him. His heart thumped hard. Phantom pain circled behind the wall of his chest. His fingers curled as his muscles locked. Vyroth closed his eyes. He didn't want to let her go. He wanted her to remain where she was—snug in his embrace, nestled against him, her cheek pressed to his. But as she turned in his arms and set her hands on his chest, he knew what she wanted.

Didn't take a genius to figure out.

Without words, she asked for space. A little breathing room. Time to think about her reaction, and what was happening to her body with him so close.

Her confusion pained him.

He longed to explain, but knew it was too soon. Too soon for her to hear about energy-fuse. Too soon for her to accept the magical bond between a Dragonkind male and his mate. Too soon for her comprehend the power of the connection.

So, when she applied pressure, pressing him back, Vyroth shifted without hesitation. He murmured her name. Eyelashes shielding her gaze, she sidestepped, moving from between him and the countertop. The gap between him and his female widened. His heart reacted, contracting as he forced himself to remain perfectly still.

Following her retreat wasn't a good idea, but...

Goddess help him.

He wanted her so badly. Needed his hands on her skin. Yearned for the taste of her on his tongue and her surrounding him. The instant he met her, she'd become his addiction. Now, the idea of her in his bed, splayed in supplication beneath him, taunted him. Haunting every waking moment.

She moved further away.

His hands twitched.

Vyroth held his ground, refusing to pursue. Accepting him was Nicole's decision. Hers alone to make.

Rushing her wasn't an option. He didn't want to be that male. Pushy and self-serving. Needy and impatient. He'd already taken once—when he'd fed inside the prison cell. He couldn't do it again. He must think of her first. She mattered more than the primal need driving him. No matter how desperate his desire for her, he refused to force the issue.

Nicole would come to him when ready. Willingly, or not at all.

For the first time in his life, he prayed energy-fuse was as strong as he'd been led to believe. He shouldn't doubt it. He'd heard about the intense bond all his life. Read about it too. Countless volumes in the lair library told interesting tales on the subject. Not that he'd needed to flip through those volumes to understand. Not with a living example inside the Scottish lair.

His aunt and uncle had provided all the evidence he required. Vyroth remembered watching the pair as a child and knew the gifts of energy-fuse—fierce loyalty, unfailing love, the savage need to be together… all the time.

He already felt the heady force of it for Nicole.

He saw the same need for him reflected in her eyes.

Hope spiraled through him. Her attraction to him—and his to her—was unmatched. The bond had taken hold. Already burned deep, wide and true. Was simply too powerful for either of them to resist for long.

Sooner rather than later, Nicole would give in to the pull. Curiosity would propel her, love would make her stay. His job was to be patient. Help her understand. Encourage her to explore. Wait for her to make the first move. Energy-fuse would do the rest, strengthening the bond minute-by-minute, hour-by-hour, every day and each night.

Flexing his hands, Vyroth opened his eyes.

Despite the pain—the gut-wrench of longing—he knew he was lucky. One of the most fortunate males of his kind. The goddess had done him a good turn, putting him in Nicole's path.

Most warriors never experienced such luck. Many searched for years, and never found their mate. Spent centuries alone. Hunted night in and night out, wishing, hoping, dreaming of the night he'd meet the female made and meant for him. More often than not, the universe dicked around. He exhaled through his nose. The fickle bitch—brutal, destructive, uncaring, denying Dragonkind the kind of love humans took for granted every day.

Vyroth refused to do the same.

Now that he'd found Nicole, he must do everything possible to keep her. If that meant enduring days—weeks, months—of denial to ensure her certainty and a lifetime of happiness, so be it. Nothing else to do. Tangled up in her, her welfare took a back seat to his, which meant—

"Vyroth."

Soft voice calling him.

Small hand sliding into his, calming him.

His whole body reacted, tightening with the need to touch. "*Tazleiah*, careful. I'm wound tight."

"I know," she whispered, tugging him away from the stove. "Relax, honey. I'm not saying no, but you've got blood all over your face."

Not saying no?

The promise simmered through him.

His brows collided. *Not saying no.*

What did that mean? Did she mean... would she... bloody hell. The idea she might want him dismantled his control. His mind took flight. Images of her beneath him streamed into his head. Heat spiked. Need went cataclysmic, burning through his veins.

His gaze sharpened on her. "Say again?"

"It's strange, I know. I feel like I shouldn't, but..." she paused.

He hung on the edge, clinging to restraint. Waiting for her to clarify. Starving. Needing. *Wanting.*

Her hand flexed in his. "I want you too, Vyroth, but the blood needs to—"

A growl rumbled out of his chest. He couldn't help it. The thought of her wanting him—being brave enough to admit it out loud—lit a fire inside him. Hellfire. She wanted him. *Wanted him,* and he needed to please her. He'd do anything his female required, and Nicole hadn't asked for much. She wanted him to wash up before...

Before.

Before.

Before.

With a quick jerk, he yanked her toward him. Her body banged into his. Ignoring her gasp, he turned toward the sink. He tossed the colander full of pasta onto the counter. Noodles went flying. Nicole huffed, the beginnings a smile playing at the corners of her mouth as he flipped on the spigot and stuck his head under the spray.

"Towel, lass. Hurry."

Body in full riot, Vyroth scrubbed the blood from his hair and beard. As the water turned pink and swirled down the drain, he traced the cut from his temple over his eye. Almost fully healed, edges knitting together with precision. Nothing left but a thin line on his skin. All thanks to Nicole. Her energy kept his magic humming, allowing him to heal faster than usual.

Cupboard doors snap open and bang closed.

He kept washing, erasing every last trace of blood.

"Here." A thick hand towel appeared in his periphery.

Turning off the water, he grabbed her offering. A fast tousle of terrycloth over his wet hair. A quick toss of the towel to one side. Raking long strands out of his face, he hooked his arm around Nicole. He lifted her off her feet. She grabbed hold and, making room for him between her thighs, buried her hands in his wet hair. He moved in, pressing his erection to the heat of her.

She made a noise in the back of her throat.

The needy sound fueled him as he spun, set her arse on the island, raised his head and—

Her mouth met his.

Fuck. His female.

No shyness. Zero hesitation. So beautiful in her acceptance of him.

Deep in his arms, Nicole didn't waste time. She nipped his bottom lip, demanding access. He opened his mouth and groaned as she sank deep, tangling her tongue with his, delivering her taste, becoming acquainted with his as she took control of the kiss.

She dragged him deep.

And held him there, a prisoner of desire, addicted to the feel of her.

Drunk on her, Vyroth ran his hands over her, dipping beneath her top, learning the shape of her. Soft skin. Gorgeous curves. Hot kisses. Burning desire, passion unleashed. Nicole kissed him like she might die if she didn't. He loved every second, but... shite, he needed to put the brakes on and slow her down.

He didn't want fast.

Not the first time.

He wanted to go gentle. Give her his time and attention. All she deserved. But as she yanked his shirt up, skimming her hands over his back, raking him gently with her nails, he lost control, forgot all about his program and got on board with hers.

20

───────

Fast was good. Quick was great. Mind scorching hot was even better.

The first time anyway.

She didn't want to wait. Or think. Bad memories might surface, and Nicole refused to let anything come between her and Vyroth. Not with his hands on her skin and his taste in her mouth. Prudence was no doubt a good idea. Sanity tried to tell her so. The heat of him, the sheer beauty of the man in her arms, shoved all thoughts of stopping aside.

A terrible decision.

Maybe.

Probably.

Nicole didn't care. She didn't want to stop. Wanted Vyroth too badly to think about consequences that might crop up in the aftermath.

Her reaction to him surprised her.

Fair or not, she'd decided to stroke men off her list. Tossed all thought of them aside, relegating one and all to the scrap heap. Vyroth changed her mind. One gentle touch led into another, firing her imagination, turning her around, bringing her to the brink.

A strange thing to admit.

After the last month, all that time spent inside a prison cell, she never thought she'd want to spend time with a man again. And sex? Forget it. No need to think about getting hot and heavy. No need to worry about clean sheets or a bikini wax. But with Vyroth in her arms, his taste in her mouth, his heat pressed hard against hers, priorities changed. In a hurry.

She'd gone from cold to hard simmer. Now, she boiled beneath the surface, needing more, desperate to explore the promise of him.

Now.

Before he slowed her down.

And he was trying. To gentle the kiss. To gentle her need. To *gentle* her.

Too bad... for him... given she wasn't on board with his plan.

Hands in his hair, she shifted on the countertop, pulling him closer. He murmured against her mouth. She wrapped her legs around his hips. He kissed her harder. A sharp nip of his teeth. Hot friction. Beautiful oblivion. Shockingly good as she grew bolder. Rolling her hips, riding the ridge of his erection, she tangled her tongue with his, stoking his fire, drawing him deeper.

He groaned.

She pressed her advantage, and with a quick tug, unzipped her hoodie. He pulled back a little. Breathing hard, lips brushing hers, he growled her name.

She shrugged out of the sweatshirt. Panting, she let it fall behind her and started working on her shirt. "Too many clothes, Vyroth. I have too many—"

"Hellfire, baby. I'm trying tae be gentle. I'm trying tae—"

"Later. Take your time later. Right now, I need to feel you. All of you."

"Niki."

"Please," she whispered, struggling to get her long-sleeved tee off.

Her plea worked.

Baring his teeth, he bit her bottom lip. The love bite propelled her higher. She squirmed, trying to kiss him and undress at the same time.

He grabbed the hem. "Arms up."

She obeyed, raising her hands.

He whipped her shirt over her head. His hands landed lightly on her skin. As she moaned in relief, he pressed her backward. Her spine met the countertop. A shiver rolled through her as he looked at her, memorizing her, devouring her with his eyes as he stroked over her bra, between her breasts, over her ribcage.

Arching into each caress, needing his touch more than she wanted her next breath, she yanked at her jeans. The top button popped. Standing between her thighs, he ignored her silent message and pressed in, spreading her thighs wider. His heat hit her. She undulated, encouraging him as he yanked at her bra. Lace slid down, cupping the undersides of her breasts, offering twin peaks a second before his mouth found her.

Hot breath engulfed her.

Shimmering eyes met hers.

She whispered his name, pleading for relief.

With a hum, Vyroth licked over her nipple, then sucked. Hard. Nicole writhed, twisting beneath him as pleasure spiraled, clawing through her. She burned and begged, losing track of everything but the hard suction. His mouth left her. She whimpered in protest, but she needn't have worried. Rolling the wet peak with his fingers, he captured its twin, bathing her in heat, making delight rise so sharply muscles inside her contracted.

Scraping her with his teeth, he sucked on her skin. Pain pinched. Satisfaction thumped through her. Oh, yeah. That was going to leave a mark. A lovely little bruise. A reminder of his possession. Something for her to admire later and—

He licked over the tiny wound.

Burying her hands in his hair, Nicole tipped her head back, needing him to take more. Everything. Whatever he wanted and... man. He was unbelievable. So good. Beautiful, gentle-rough, in no way sweet.

Just the way she wanted him.

"Lift your hips."

Another command.

Nicole didn't hesitate. She lifted as he unzipped her jeans and tugged. Denim slid down her thighs. With a yank, he freed one of her legs. He grabbed the sides of her underwear. A sharp jerk. The sound of tearing fabric, then nothing. She was bare, completely exposed, nowhere to hide.

Not that she wanted to. With him looming over her, she needed something, but escape wasn't it.

Watching him from beneath her lashes, she cocked her knee. Eyes aglow, bathing her in blue and violet shimmer, he drew a sharp breath. His tongue touched his bottom lip as she ignored the drag of her jeans on one ankle and opened wide, offering him all of her.

His fingers flexed on her thighs. He pushed her legs even wider. "Fucking gorgeous, lass."

Holding her gaze, his fingers slid through her wet.

She made a greedy sound as he circled her clit.

Still fully clothed, he spread her open, pressed in, playing, searching for pleasure points as he watched her react. Nicole didn't hold back. She gave him everything. Allowed him to see. Showed him how his touch made her feel, how much she wanted him. No shyness. Zero deception. Complete honesty, nothing hidden.

Pushing two fingers deep, he stroked her from the inside out. Gentle touch. Perfect rhythm. Deep and beautiful. His mouth joined the party, landing at the top of her mound. Shoving her legs wider, he rolled the flat of his tongue over her sex.

Muscles tightened around his fingers. Her eyelashes fluttered. "More."

"Greedy," he growled against her.

Another wicked lick over the heart of her. His hum of satisfaction rippled through her. The vibration nearly sent her soaring. Tittering on the edge, she tilted her hips, rolling into each stroke. Hungry, he ate her, licking deeper, fingers thrusting, ratcheting up the pressure.

She bucked.

"Amazing. Taste so fucking good, Niki."

"Vyroth, please, I'm close. So—"

He stopped teasing and, working her hard, sucked her clit into his mouth. His teeth grazed her. Heels digging into his shoulders, she hit the high note. Her spine arched. Her lungs locked. Nicole rasped his name as she flew out of the kitchen into rapture, coming so hard she lost everything but the feel of his hand holding her down.

Gasping, still convulsing, she clung to Vyroth, trusting him to keep her safe as he licked over her nipple, making it burn as he set himself against her entrance. Without waiting, he pushed deep. Pleasure hammered her. She came again, twisting as he pulled back and thrust forward, making her mew as he started loving her. No finesse. No control. A guy on the edge, no intention of slowing down.

She didn't want him to. He felt fantastic. Long and thick as he rode her hard and fast.

Shoving his arm under her hips, he changed the angle of his strokes.

"Yesss," she hissed, holding on tight, moving with him. "Yes, honey. You feel beautiful. So beautiful inside me."

"Niki. Niki." Cupping the nape of her neck, he kept her where he wanted her. Belly sliding against hers, he raised his head. Shimmering eyes met and held hers as he rocked in, retreated and came back, holding her immobile, taking what he needed. "Gorgeous, baby. Go again."

"No." Lungs hitching, she shuddered. "Too much."

Gaze hot on her, he upped the pace, riding wilder. "Come again, Niki."

Sliding on the countertop, she shook her head.

"Aye, you can."

"Honey."

"Again." Releasing her hip, he slid his hand over her belly. Down and in. His thumb hit the spot and circled. Bliss jolted through her as his strokes went from long and hard to short, strong jabs. The tip of him rubbed a sensitive spot inside her. She jerked against him. He thrust, firm and determined, hitting the spot over and over.

She spiraled out of control.

He grunted. "Aye, baby. Let go. Give it tae me one more time."

Unable to do anything else, she fell over the edge

into orgasm. Head thrown back, she keened, contracting around him. He pulsed deep inside her and, groaning her name, folded forward. Face pressed to throat, chest brushing hers, he held her tight, gathering up all her shattered pieces, keeping her safe as she drifted weightless, carried on a wave of bliss.

21

He needed to re-evaluate the plan. Cutting his hair was no longer a good idea. The long strands might drive him crazy, constantly falling in his eyes, but Nicole loved it. Vyroth drifted deeper into relaxation as she played, threading her fingers through his dark locks, caressing him with lazy strokes. Her nails scraped his scalp every second or third pass, making him purr.

The sound came from deep inside his chest.

Pure contentment.

One of her hands left his hair to trail over his shoulder.

Vyroth sighed, reveling in the caress, and stayed right where he was—bent over the island, snug in her arms, deep between her thighs.

Felt so good to have her hands on him.

Felt better to be buried inside her.

So crazy good, he didn't want to pull out.

He pressed forward instead, nudging deeper, hearing her gasp, feeling her hands fist in his hair. Her hips rocked as she squirmed beneath him. He'd called it right. She was *greedy*. Needy, ready for another go, even after he'd made her come three times to his one.

Boded well for his future. He could ride her all day, and Nicole wouldn't complain. She'd meet him. Match him. Demand her due. All he could give her, then ask for more.

Beautiful female.

His mate.

Perfect for him.

Grateful for the gift of her, he worked his mouth against her throat. Soft kisses. A gentle lick, feeding her pleasure, sipping at her energy, replenishing his strength.

Nicole hummed. "We going again?"

"Eventually."

"I tire you out?" she asked, a teasing lilt in her tone.

Raising his head, he planted a forearm on the counter and smiled at her. "Food first, lass. Then I'll fuck you again."

Her mouth curved up at the corners. "Yippee."

He ran his gaze over her face. Expression open. Eyes lit with happiness. Body relaxed as she toyed with the ends of his hair. None of the stress that had plagued her since leaving the underground prison. Anxiety gone. He released a breath. Free and clear of the shitstorm. His mate had crossed over, allowing him to help her get past the first hurdle—accepting him sexually.

Caressing her in return, he cupped her cheek, brushing thick bangs out of her eyes. Transfixed by her soft skin, he traced the line of freckles over her nose. Content. Relaxed. Waiting on him to move, happy for him to stay deep inside her.

Unable to help himself, he leaned in. His mouth brushed hers. She opened, drawing him in to dueling tongues and decadent tastes. He kissed her slowly, taking his time, pleasing her, learning the subtle nuances that made up Nicole.

With a nip, he drew away and stood, pulling her with him. "Food, lass."

Sitting on the edge of the counter, she ran her hands along his jaw, down the sides of his neck as he pulled out, leaving the warm cove of her body. She sucked in a quick breath. The sharp noise sounded like a protest.

"All right?" Hands on her hips, he kissed her temple, holding still until she steadied.

Color burnished her cheeks as Nicole nodded.

Seeing the blush, Vyroth stroked her jaw. "What?"

"Don't like losing you."

His chest tightened. Hellfire. She was honest. Unable to shield herself. Unwilling to give him less than a mate deserved. Even though she had no idea what that meant. Another reason he'd fallen fast and hard for her.

Dipping his head, he treated himself to another kiss, then hooked his fingers in her bra. Seeing the small mark on the curve of her breast, pride rolled through him. His whisker burns on her skin. His love bite beneath the lace she wore. Nicole was now *his*, in every way a female could belong to a male.

His dragon cuffed in satisfaction.

Drawing his thumb over the tiny bruise, Vyroth silently agreed. Bloody hell, he was proud. Proud of Nicole's bravery. Proud of her intelligence and fortitude. Proud to call her his own.

Cupping her breast, he held her a moment, then drew the lace up and covered her. With a murmur, he conjured his clothes. Faded Levi's settled around his waist, cupping his arse and legs. His favorite Mötley Crüe tee settled in his hand. Drawing it over her head, he helped Nicole shrug it on. Soft cotton fell to her thighs as he stepped back and lifted her off the island.

Her jeans rolled off her ankle and hit the floor.

Something flew out of the pocket, clattering across tile.

"Crap," she said, bending to pick up the small, black stick. "I forgot about that."

"What is it?"

"Flash drive… for a computer. I'm supposed to give it to you."

"Where'd you get it?"

"Lapier gave it to me," she said, offering it to him. "He's the one who broke me out. Told me to get to you. Set up everything. Gave me the keycode to your cell, left the canoe and… well. You know the rest."

Thank fuck for Lapier. He owed the male a debt of gratitude.

"Lapier one of Montgomery's crew?"

The name made her stiffen.

Regret clawed through him. Shite. He shouldn't have mentioned the bastard. The last thing Nicole needed was to be reminded. Especially now, after she'd given herself to him, been so intimate, trusted him with so much.

"Sorry, Niki," he said, gathering her hair in his hand. Soft strands tangled around his fingers as he drew the dark mass over her shoulder. Caressing her nape, he sent magic swirling down her spine, using his touch to soothe her. "I didnae think."

A furrow between her brows, she chewed on her bottom lip. "It's all right. Tiptoeing around it won't help. Never does. At some point, we'll need to talk about what happened."

"Whenever you're ready, lass."

Light brown eyes met his. She studied him a moment. "You already know, don't you? You've been inside my head."

"On the flight here," he said, unwilling to lie. The truth would serve her better. Help him to start knitting her back together. Refusing to look away, he played with the ends of her long hair. "You were stressed, reliving it and I—"

"Took it away. Helped me go to sleep."

"Aye."

Stepping into him, she pressed her cheek to his chest. Fingers threaded through his belt loops, she hugged him. "Thank you."

"Brave lass," he whispered into the top of her head, undone by her. Humbled by the strength of her. Most females would turn away, try to forget, brave the future without acknowledging the wound. He understood the need. Trauma kicked everyone's arse. Was never easy. Pain tore people apart, but... his mate was different. She tackled it head-on, deciding to face the hurt instead of turning away. "You make me so bloody proud."

Tucked in tight, she gave him a squeeze. "Lapier's a prisoner. A Numbai. He doesn't want to be there anymore than we did."

Turning the drive over in his hand, Vyroth frowned. "You know what's on it?"

"No, but he said it's important. That you and your pack need it. That once you broke the encryption, you'd know what to do with the information."

A mystery.

A fucked up one Vyroth knew must be investigated... immediately.

Numbai didn't screw around.

Caretakers of Dragonkind, males like Lapier took the oath to serve and protect seriously. No wiggle room for that race. Just straight up devotion. Which meant whatever was on the drive had the potential to upend lives. Montgomery's? Maybe. But instinct warned Vyroth to be careful. Something about the cloak and dagger bothered him. Numbai weren't stupid. Lapier would've waited for the right moment, the right warrior, to ensure the drive—and whatever bombshell was embedded on it—ended up in responsible hands.

His attention tracked to the phone sitting on the countertop.

Two empty bowls sat beside it. Sauce bubbled inside the lone pot on the stove, throwing steam, reminding him of his original plan.

Phone call first.

Eat, shower, love Nicole into a pleasure coma second.

"Dish up, Niki." Snaking an arm around her, he walked her toward the stove. As he came abreast of it, he grabbed the phone. "Willnae be but a moment."

She nodded and turned to the bowls.

Tilting the cordless faceup, he dialed. Buttons beeped as he called the only number his pack kept active—the one inside at the Dragon's Horn, the pub and Scotch distillery he and his brothers owned. Calling the mountain lair would've been more effective. A faster line to Cyprus would serve him better.

Alas, not to be.

Cairngorm didn't have a phone.

The only way to reach his brother inside the mountain lair was mind-speak. Too far away to use it, he needed to pivot away from magic and kick it old school. Which left him one option—Rannock. The male stayed in Aberdeen, inside the city lair, full-time, running the distillery, overseeing the pub. Problem was, the surly SOB might not—

"What?" The rough bark blasted over the line. A nasty snarl followed. A warning to whoever had woken him. "Talk, motherfucker."

Vyroth's heart started to thump. Relief nearly flattened him as he listened to his packmate growl into the receiver. Hellfire, he missed the pissed off attitude. Missed the male. Missed all his brothers. Had longed to hear anything that reminded him of home for two very long months.

Closing his eyes, a death grip on the phone, he pressed his free hand to the countertop. He needed something solid. Something to ground and steady him. After a second, he managed to find his voice. "Ran, man."

A pause. Some rustling. A loud thump, then...

"Vyroth?"

"Aye, brother. It's me."

"Shite, lad," Rannock said, sounding both irritated and relieved. "Where you been? Cyprus is losing his mind. You good? All in one piece?"

He smiled. Trust Rannock to snarl while concerned. "All limbs attached and working. I'm good now, Ran, but I haven't been for a while."

"Tell me."

"Long story. I'll fill you in when you get here."

"Where's here?"

"Cologne," he said, watching Nicole pour sauce and meatballs over noodles. "I need you tae get the lads moving. Need you mobile asap."

"We going hunting?"

"Aye."

"Target?"

"A mercenary. I want him put down."

"Understood. On it." The thud of boots came through the line. "Address."

Vyroth rattled off directions to the safehouse.

"Got it."

"Oh, and Ran... one more thing."

"Shoot."

"Got precious cargo with me, so don't screw around. Get here fast, bring as many brothers as you can."

"A female," Rannock murmured. "She yours?"

"Aye."

"Seems to be going around. Everybody's catching it... like the fucking flu."

Vyroth's brows collided. "What?"

"Nothing, 'cept things are moving and shaking here. Bad mojo, laddie. Cy'll tell you when he sees you," Rannock said as a door slammed somewhere near him. "Anything else?"

Moving and shaking? Bad mojo?

Vyroth scowled into the phone. What the hell did that mean? He wanted to ask, but didn't bother. Rannock never said more than he wanted to, and given the amount of sunlight hitting the bank of magic-fueled, fast darkening windows, trying to pull it out of the stubborn SOB would waste time he didn't have.

"I'm traveling with another male," he said, thinking about Tempel. "He's solid. Skilled. Try not to kill him when you get here."

"Make no promises..." Rannock trailed off, waiting.

Vyroth finished his buddy's favorite saying. "Tell no lies."

"Believe it, brother. Stay cool. Keep it tight. We'll be on our way in less than an hour."

He opened his mouth to say thanks.

The phone clicked.

Dead air replaced Rannock's voice on the line.

His mouth curved. Another thing he missed—the brusque efficiency of his pack. Nothing his brothers-in-arms loved more than a good fight. The promise of one always perked his packmates up and... no wonder Rannock ended the conversation sounding almost happy. The bad-tempered male lived for action. Vyroth didn't blame him. Not much happened in Scotland. Other Dragonkind skirted the island, giving it a wide berth, staying off his pack's radar. A smart move, given he and his brothers didn't like interlopers.

Any warrior brave enough to enter their territory never left that way.

In truth, none of the bastards ever left at all.

"Everything okay?" Nicole asked, handing him a bowl piled high with pasta.

"Backup's on the way."

"Good."

Sure was... very good. Time wasn't on his side. He needed Cyprus and the lads to arrive before sundown. Otherwise, Montgomery would slither away, find a rock, crawl under it and hide, before Vyroth got another chance to sink his claws into him.

22

The voice tugged at his temples. Surfacing from the fog of sleep, Vyroth opened his eyes. Blurry shapes above him. Soft mattress underneath him. Warm female curled around him. Sweet scent. Soft skin. Tendrils of long dark hair tangled across his chest.

He blinked.

The ceiling inside the bedroom Nicole chose came into focus. Dark wood. Ancient coffers with hand-painted murals inside each square. Pretty, but not his style. He would've preferred the room decorated in medieval weaponry. His lips twitched as he recalled his mate's reaction to it. She'd made a face, then given him attitude, refusing to sleep next to a guillotine.

Turning his face into her hair, he breathed her in. Sweet. Amazing. She smelled like apples and cinnamon—the shampoo in the shower—and him, a fantastic combination. He hummed, shifting as his body went from half-mast to fully awake, wanting another taste of her.

He slid his hand over her lower back.

Naked beneath the blankets with him, she didn't move. Not surprising after the day she shared with him. She hadn't gotten much sleep. He'd kept her up, shunning shut-eye in favor of hot, mind-blowing sex. He almost felt bad about that. Nicole needed sleep, but he hadn't been able to leave her alone. Driven by compulsion, he explored every inch of her, learning her shape, finding her hotspots, committing her to memory. Now, he knew her by heart, every beautiful curve, inside and out.

Careful not to wake her, he turned from his back onto his side. Soft skin brushed his palms as he stroked her back. His hand drifted over her bottom. She shifted in sleep, hitching her knee over his hip. Trailing his mouth over her bare shoulder, he—

A hiss swirled against his temples.

A growl followed, thumping the inside of his skull.

"Brother, stop messing around." Tingled with impatience, his twin's voice sawed through mind-speak. *"Answer."*

His mouth curved. Vyroth linked in, completing the connection. *"Here, Cy."*

"Roll yer sorry arse out of bed, buddy," Tydrin said, tone filled with gravel. *"We're ten minutes out."*

Ten minutes? Already? Shite, his brothers were fast. Hadn't messed around getting out of Scotland.

"What time is it?"

"Nearly four-thirty," Rannock said, the sound of rotor blades in the background.

"Ran, you in the Hog?*"* he asked, referring to his packmate's favorite toy—a helicopter he'd stolen from a decommissioned army base in Former Soviet Union.

Rannock grunted. *"What you think?"*

"Right." Shouldn't have asked. He already knew the answer. Combine the chop coming through mind-speak with the fact Rannock was well, *Rannock*, and the outcome wasn't difficult to determine. The male

never missed an opportunity to take his baby out for a spin.

A relic from the Cold War, the helicopter sat twelve passengers... easy. And that was before Rannock stole it. Now, the thing was a beast. New interior. Pristine paint job. Supercharged turboshaft engines that made the Hog so fast top brass in the United Kingdom would salivate if the bastards ever managed to get eyeballs on it.

"Land in the back garden, Ran."

"Roger that."

"Meet us there," Cyprus said, sounding pissed off. Understandable. His twin didn't enjoy the Hog nearly as much as Rannock. *"Gonna need some cloud cover."*

The understatement of the year.

With the sun shining, his pack couldn't exit the helicopter without suffering the effects. Burnt skin was the least of it. After what happened to Wallaig, Vyroth worried more about their eyes. He didn't need his brothers injured and half-blind when he went into battle tonight. The lads needed to be in tip-top shape for him to get a bead on Montgomery and take out his crew.

Thinking about cloud cover, Vyroth shifted away from Nicole. *"On it."*

Careful not to wake her, he slid toward the edge of the bed. She grumbled in protest. Her brow puckered as his hands left her. With a murmur, he gave her a pillow to nestle into instead of him. She grabbed hold and snuggled in. Not wanting to leave her, he lingered. Eyes on her face, he tucked the duvet around her to ensure she stayed warm.

Standing beside the bed, he conjured his clothes. Jeans and another of his favorite tees settled on his body. Black motorcycle boots went on his feet.

Crossing the room, he grabbed the door handle, then paused to look at her over his shoulder. Sleeping hard, snug beneath the blankets. Curled around his pillow. Dark hair in a riot, silken strands flowing across white sheets.

He exhaled long and slow.

All good. No need to worry.

Dragon half restless and waiting, he conjured clean clothes for her. Athletic wear, soft, warm, comfortable, for her to pull on when she woke. Leaving the stack folded on the nightstand, he pulled the door open and, stepping into the hallway, closed it softly behind him.

Footfalls sounded to his right.

Coming down from the third floor, Tempel walked off the last step.

Vyroth tipped his chin in greeting, then got a load of the male's face. He stopped short. The fine hair on his nape stood on end. Not good. Something was up. Or had gone terribly wrong. Boots planted on the area rug, he stared at Tempel. Instinct sharpened. Perception expanded. Magic crackled as he read and analysed the situation.

Jaw set. Worry in his eyes. Tense verging on upset.

"What's wrong?"

Tempel rolled his shoulders, trying to work out his tension. "I can't reach my commander."

"That unusual?"

"Very."

"How many times have you called?"

"Been trying all day." White-knuckling a cordless phone, Tempel lifted it... and Vyroth waited. For his friend to let loose, let fly and hurl the annoying piece of technology against the wall. Eyes shimmering, he scowled at the buttons, then gathered his control and dropped his arm. "Nothing but crickets. It just rings and rings."

"Could be—"

"Even if he didn't make it home last night, someone should be there. Two of my packmates, at least. I'm new to the pack, but we hunt in pairs. Always. No exceptions." Dragging his attention from the phone, Tempel refocused on him. The helplessness in the male's gaze gutted him. He knew that feeling. Had struggled with hopelessness more times than he wanted to count in the last two months. "Something's wrong, Vyroth."

Steeping in close, he reached out. His hand landed on Tempel's shoulder. He squeezed, understanding, solidarity, concern in his touch. "When did you land inside the—"

"A month before you."

"Any idea why you were taken?"

Tempel shook his head. "Montgomery never said. He tasered me. Pulled me straight out of the sky. Next thing I know I'm surrounded by an electrical field deep underground and..." Confusion and fury clashed in his dark green-rimmed gaze. "Shit."

"What?" Vyroth asked, watching the male closely.

His brows furrowed. "I don't want to believe it, but I've gone over it and over it—the night I went down."

"And?"

"Achan."

"What about him?" Vyroth asked, guessing Achan was part of the Belarus pack.

"He... Vyroth... I think he might've set me up. I thought Montgomery got him too. Took him down at the same time, but I keep replaying it. Like a tape inside my head and..." Not wanting to accept his conclusion, fighting to come up with a different one, Tempel looked away. "One second, he was there—on my wing tip. The next—gone."

"He flew you into a trap?"

"Yeah. Maybe."

"You could be wrong. He could be in the prison. We may have left him behind. Mayhap..."

"No," Tempel said on a growl. "He's not there."

"You sure?"

"The earth speaks to me, man. I know exactly who's inside Montgomery's little shop of horrors. Achan isn't there."

Interesting.

Earth dragons were secretive. Privacy and seclusion came part and parcel with their antisocial natures. Most never joined a Dragonkind pack, so the information Tempel shared qualified as true revelations. Ones he knew Cyprus would want to hear. If half of what Tempel said proved true, his twin wouldn't hesitate. He'd try to steal the male away from the Belarus pack. Turn on the charm in order to convince him to join his pack in Scotland.

If that happened, Vyroth wouldn't complain.

He'd welcome Tempel with open arms. Strength. Skill. Loyalty. Qualities the male possessed in spades. A warrior of his caliber would be an excellent addition to any pack.

Add that to the fact he liked the male. Had spent hours talking to him through a wall. The connection he and Tempel shared surpassed friendship. Months of keeping each other sane inside prison had led to something else—brotherhood, the kind of bond that would never be broken.

"Fucking Achan." Tempel snarled. "I'm gonna tear his guts out and make him eat them."

Vyroth snorted. "Always good to have goals."

"I need to go home, Vyroth. Need to figure out what's going on."

"After." Understanding the urgency, he slapped his shoulder. "Hunt and kill Montgomery first, then—"

"Straight to Minsk."

"Sounds like a plan," Vyroth said, glancing toward the stairs. "I'll go with you."

"You don't have to—"

"Pull your head outta your arse, lad. No way you're going alone."

Tempel nodded, relief in his eyes.

Releasing his friend, he strode across the landing toward the stairs. "Who's your commander?"

"Ezram."

"I've heard of him."

"Most have."

"Not a favorite of the Archguard."

"Thorn in Rodin's side."

Poised on the top tread, Vyroth smiled over his shoulder. "I like him already."

Tempel's mouth curled. The tension holding him lifted as he shoved the phone in his back pocket and put himself in gear. Hot on his heel, Tempel followed him down the stairs. Lights embedded in the treads blinked on, casting the stairwell in shadows as he jogged toward the main floor.

Not that he needed the illumination.

Night vision up and running, he saw everything. High polish on the railing and banister. Worn patches on the aging runner. The ugly-as-shite paisley wallpaper above the wainscoting. Nothing escaped his attention as his magic rambled, coating the floor, lining the walls, gauging the distance between him and his brothers-in-arms.

Less than three miles away now.

Coming in hard.

Coming in fast.

Just a few minutes from touchdown.

Boots thumping on the steps, he upped his pace. Wooden treads creaked. Sound echoed through the house, spiraling behind him and up the stairwell. Rounding the last landing, he leapt over the last flight. Feet rapping across ceramic tile, he crossed the corridor and entered the kitchen.

His attention tracked to the windows.

Darkened by magic, the glass rippled, blocking out lethal UV rays.

Skirting the island, table and sectional, he stopped in front of a pair of French doors. The back wall boasted three of the suckers. When thrown open, the interior space would expand to include the back garden.

Tempel set up shop beside him. Crossing his arms, he leaned sideways. His shoulder bumped Vyroth's.

Glancing at the male, he raised a brow.

"Get any sleep?" he asked, the devil in his eyes.

Vyroth went cold. Electricity crackled over his shoulders. "Watch it."

"Or what?"

"I'll rearrange your face." He bared his teeth, warning his friend off the subject. He didn't care that Tempel was teasing. He wasn't like other males. He never talked. What he did to Nicole in bed was off limits. His protective nature, thoughts of his mate, made him double down on the conviction.

No one but him would ever know the incredible beauty of Nicole in his arms.

Tempel grinned. "Gotta say, man. Like your style."

"Good to know. Still—"

"What?"

"Bugger off."

Worry on the back burner, his friend threw his head back and laughed.

Vyroth flexed his hands, tamping down the need to knock Tempel's teeth down his throat. Hitting the jackass wouldn't get him anywhere. Except, maybe, into a knock down, drag out fight. An intriguing notion. Brawling with Tempel would be fun. The male knew how to handle himself. Would give as good as he got. Something to explore, but…

Some other time.

Right now, his brothers-in-arms needed cover.

Taking a deep breath, Vyroth called on his ability to manipulate the weather. His dragon half answered with storm clouds. Thick, impenetrable, sun-killing murk rolled overhead. Thunder rumbled. Lightning struck beyond the windows. Reacting to the absence of sunlight, glass panes lightened, allowing electro-static current and storm flash into the room.

Turning his head to protect his eyes from the light, Tempel took a step back. "They landing in the back garden?"

"Aye."

"I'll open the portal."

With a murmured 'thanks,' Vyroth kept the storm glow snapping, thickening the thunderclouds as he heard the chop of rotor blades. Air displaced, whipping across the garden. Treetops whipped. Dead leaves whirled up outdoor steps and across the stone patio. Debris battered the windows as Rannock set the huge helicopter down on muted winter grass.

His heart thumped the inside of his chest.

His skin prickled as the urge to rush outside hit him.

Strung tight, Vyroth planted his feet and held his

ground. Greeting his packmates the way he wanted to would only slow them down. No matter how thick the cloud cover, none of his brothers relished the idea of being outside during the day. Toss in the fact Cyprus wouldn't give him a free pass and... aye. He needed a minute to prepare.

For whatever Cyprus decided to dish out.

Whatever that ended up being, he'd accept it. He deserved every bit of his twin's anger. He'd made huge mistakes. Too many to count. Now, he must atone. Make it right with his brothers and apologize for leaving Aberdeen without back-up. For pulling a disappearing act that lasted months. For worrying the warriors who loved him, always had his back, and dropped everything to reach him when he called.

23

———

Voices in the hall outside the bedroom door woke her. She heard floorboards creak and deep baritones. Hushed. Vocal resonance muted. A conversation held in indistinct undertones. Curled around a pillow, warm beneath a thick duvet, Nicole listened a moment, tracking the whispers.

Two guys talking, trying to be quiet.

Opening her eyes, she blinked sleep away and searched for an alarm clock.

Nothing on the bedside table nearest her.

Turning beneath the sheets, she glanced toward the other one. No clock there either, just a pile of folded clothes. She stared at the neat stack a moment before it hit her. Her lips tipped up. Vyroth. Beautiful man. Gorgeous spirit. He'd held her close while she slept. Cuddled with her in between bouts of life-affirming sex, chatting about everything from his family in Scotland to his favorite color.

Natural. No awkwardness. Endlessly comfortable in himself, confident in her.

As though she was a natural extension of him. As though she'd been with him all her life. Like she belonged right where she'd chosen to be—in his arms.

Such a revelation.

He was a charming epiphany. A wake-up call on so many levels.

She'd heard of love at first sight. Her sister was a big believer in the aftershocks. The pinpricks of kismet (providence, destiny... whatever. Call it what you wanted.) when a woman met the right man. Discounting Cate's theory, Nicole scoffed whenever her sister waxed poetic, dreaming about *one day*—the instant she collided with the man meant for her and the connection went stratospheric.

Nicole pursed her lips.

Well, she wasn't scoffing now.

The past day with Vyroth changed everything. Her outlook along with her understanding of how love and relationships worked.

People had no idea what it felt like to be struck by, well... lightning.

Seriously.

No idea.

But as she lay in bed listening to Vyroth and Tempel talk in the hallway, she *knew*. Knew everything and understood more.

He hadn't hidden anything from her. Vyroth gave her what she needed. She asked. He answered. No hedging. No deflecting. Just straight-up honesty. His integrity impressed her. Her childhood, the rootless way her dad rolled through life, made things clear. She recognized Vyroth for the rarity he was. Not many people possessed enough courage to lay it all on the line. But as she listened to him explain about Dragonkind, the energy exchange and the moment he realized she was his mate, her reaction to him started to make sense.

The idea she belonged with him seemed far-fetched, but didn't feel that way. Strange but... his bond with her—the one she felt for him—didn't frighten her. Nothing she learned during the day shook her certainty.

Vyroth was right.

He belonged to her and, somewhere along the way, without meaning to, she decided she belonged to him too.

"Hell," she whispered, raking hair out of her face. "Cate's going to kill me."

Staring at the ceiling, she thought about her sister, her dad, the life she'd made for herself in Savannah, and listened as the guys moved away. She heard stair treads squeak and, mind whirling, imagined going home.

She frowned.

Home.

And it struck her.

She didn't miss Savannah. Hadn't lived there long. Felt no real connection to the city her dad had chosen to stake his claim.

Not surprising.

Forming attachments to people and places wasn't smart.

The constant moving around during childhood taught her the danger—and heartache—of making friends, only to lose them.

Her dad liked to drift, shuffling them from place to place. Onto the next mark. Away from those he drew into his cons... until he met Terry. The moment that happened, things changed for the better. After a lifetime of bouncing around, her dad settled down to build a relationship, finding honest work, managing the scrapyard, giving her and Cate a stable environment.

All right. So, it came a little late in their lives, but…

At least, he'd done it.

She'd gone to school her senior year. Managed to graduate high school. Made a few friends along the way. But now, with Vyroth firmly fixed in her picture, things would need to change. Again.

Cate wouldn't like it.

Her sister liked change about as much as wasps enjoyed being disturbed. The buzzing would be loud, an angry swarm at first, but Cate loved her. She'd come around. The biggest problem would be the Dragonkind angle.

No one could know.

Vyroth and his kind needed to stay hidden from the human world. Nothing good would come from exposing the existence of a secret race of dragon-shifters. One that, if brought into the light of day, would cause mass panic and military involvement.

A problem.

A serious one.

She hated to lie to her sister. Cate was her best friend. Astute. Relentless. So street-smart she'd know something was off when Nicole called home. Her sister's BS detector would start dinging, and one-point-five seconds later, she'd start digging, trying to figure out what Nicole wasn't telling her.

Dragging her fingers through her hair, Nicole gnawed on her lip, then glanced at the pile of clothes. Time to get up. She needed to talk to Vyroth. Wanted his take on the situation. A different angle from which to look at things. Or better yet, a plan of attack.

He knew his world better than she did. Stood to reason he'd be able to help.

Shoving the duvet aside, Nicole exited the bed. Chilly air attacked her bare skin. Ignoring the goosebumps, she grabbed the clothes and made a beeline to the bathroom. Mind locked in the logistics of falling for a man-dragon, she completed her morning routine. Teeth brushed. Face washed. Moisturizer applied. Triple elastics corralling her hair into a messy bun on top of her head.

Dressed in jogging pants, a long-sleeved tee and dark red hoodie, she hunted for her running shoes. Finding the pair under the bed, she sat down, laced up, then headed for the door. As she pulled it open and stepped into the wide central corridor, a prickle shimmied up her spine.

Her scalp tingled.

A shiver rolled through her.

Standing in the middle of an area rug, Nicole tilted her head and...

Intense hum. Nasty vibration. The buzz sawed across her skin, warning her, bringing swift understanding. Something was wrong. Vyroth was in trouble. Under threat. Surrounded by... her brows collided... something lethal.

Her head snapped toward the stairs.

Her body followed, driving her across the landing.

Nicole didn't think. She ran, heart hammering, feet pounding on treads, descending the staircase fast. Reaching the last flight, she raced down the steps, across the hall, straight into—

Mayhem.

Complete and total chaos.

Her brain took a quick snapshot. Two guys fighting. Vyroth and some other man locked in mortal combat. Pieces of broken furniture on the floor. Dents in the wall next to the archway. Couch cushions thrown everywhere. Fists flying. Feet kicking. Grunts, curses, snarls echoed inside the great room. While three other men she didn't know stood off to one side watching.

Eyes trained on the fight, Nicole put on the brakes. Rubber treads squeaking across kitchen tile, she slid to a stop beside the island.

Arms crossed, leaning back gainst the countertop, Tempel smiled at her. "Evenin', darlin'."

"What the hell?"

"Reunion."

She threw him an incredulous look. "What?"

"Brotherly love," he said, a gleeful look in his eyes. "Scots really know how to live."

She opened her mouth. Closed again. A second later, her brain kicked back into gear and she yelled, "Vyroth! Stop it! Stop—"

Tempel pushed away from counter. "Stay out of it, Niki."

"Are you crazy? They're going to kill each other."

"Nah. Nothing but love taps."

A crash sounded.

The walls shuddered as pieces of the stone fireplace flew into the air.

Nicole moved to stop the fight.

Tempel stepped into her path. Blocking her view, arms spread wide, he herded her backward, toward the pantry. "You hungry? I'm thinking pancakes. You like pancakes?"

Pancakes?

Nicole scowled at him.

Vyroth and his brother were tearing each other apart, and Tempel wanted to make *pancakes*. The guy was bent. Off the rails. Twisted or something. His reaction didn't make sense. No way should he look calm, happy even, while two men destroyed his house in a crazy dragon ritual designed to... well, she didn't know exactly. But as the cursing intensified, fists cracked against bone and the house shook, Nicole knew whatever it meant wasn't the least bit good.

24

Fists at the ready, guard up, Vyroth dipped beneath his brother's punch. The right hook whiffed over his head. Aggression set to maximum, he dodged an elbow, then powered up and hammered Cyprus in the side. A crack ripped through the room as his knuckles slammed into his twin's ribcage. With a grunt, his brother stumbled backward, past the table toward the couch.

Vyroth lunged after him.

No sense sitting back. Waiting for his twin to recover wasn't in his playbook. Giving up the advantage—even for a split second—would give his twin the upper hand.

Ramming his shoulder into his brother's chest, he hit Cyprus again.

With a curse, his brother careened into the sectional.

Grabbing hold, Vyroth wrapped him up and, driving with his legs, lifted, smashing Cyprus into the couch. The frame cracked. Wood bent. He and Cyprus sailed over the square back, bounced on seat cushions and, with a thud, landed on the floor.

Wooden floorboards shook.

The coffee table pinwheeled, glass top exploding as it crashed into the hearth. Jagged splinters flew into the air. Chunks of stone fireplace followed, bashing into the flat screen mounted above the mantel. The thing listed sideways, then toppled, falling face-first toward the floor.

Letting go of his brother, Vyroth rolled one way.

Cyprus rolled the other and—

Crash!

The TV shattered as it collided face-first with the floor.

Grinning like a lunatic, Cyprus gained his feet and dove over the fractured screen.

Ready for the move, Vyroth met him halfway, grappling as his twin drove him spine first into the wall. Plaster cracked. Dust puffed into a white cloud, raining down, getting in his eyes as he wrapped his leg around the back of his brother's knee. He shoved. Cyprus tripped, reeling backward, taking fistfuls of his shirt with him.

Cotton ripped.

Vyroth laughed.

He loved sparing with his twin. Enjoyed pitting his skills against a male who not only knew him, but shared his DNA. Strength pitted against strength. Lethal intent met by brutal intensity. Beautiful and fierce. Will and wits bracketed by the need to win. The fact Cyprus fought dirty only added spice to the game.

And right now, his brother craved the game. Needed to exorcize his worry. To make sure Vyroth was all right. To see and feel it for himself.

Vyroth understood the compulsion. Had Cyprus disappeared, no word for months on end, he'd want reassurances too.

Regaining his balance, Cyprus reengaged.

He spun away from the wall and, dodging another strike, slammed his elbow into Cyprus's side. Nailing him in the ribs again. Same spot. Already sore from the first blow he unleashed.

His twin cursed.

Someone behind him yelled.

Deep in the fight, it took a second for him to understand.

He glanced toward the kitchen—

Cyprus unpackaged an uppercut beneath his chin.

His head snapped back. As he stumbled, his gaze caught on Nicole. Pale face. Wide eyes. Fear for him in her scent.

He snarled at his brother.

Bloody knuckles raised to hit him again, Cyprus pulled his punch. Shimmering violet eyes met his as his twin fired up mind-speak. *"Your mate."*

"Aye." Flexing his hand, Vyroth dropped his guard. *"She doesnae understand."*

"My mate wouldnae either."

Vyroth blinked. *"What?"*

"A lot's happened since you left, brother."

"You're mated?"

"Elise. My heart and soul. Gorgeous female. So beautiful she takes my breath away."

"I know the feeling."

His brother's mouth curved. *"Fantastic, isnae it?"*

Vyroth couldn't disagree. He and Nicole might be new, but what he felt for her defied reason. Logic was an afterthought. Something to mull over, then discard. He loved that Cyprus understood. No need to explain. His twin was already there, heart-deep in the female he'd made his own.

A miracle in his world.

One he now shared with his twin.

"*Fuck, Cy.*" Stepping over splintered wood, ignoring aches and pains, he reached for his brother. Grabbing hold, he embraced his twin, giving him a squeeze. "*It's good tae see you.*"

Arms wrapped around him, Cyprus hung on just as hard. "*You had me worried.*"

His throat went tight. "*Had myself worried for a while.*"

"*You sure you're good?*"

"*Aye.*"

"*Then...*" Retreating a little, Cyprus scanned his face, making sure he spoke true. His mouth tipped up at the corners, he nodded. "*Introduce me tae your mate, then fill us in. The lads are dying tae know what's going on.*"

"*Speculating?*"

Cyprus huffed. "*All kinds of wild theories.*"

Slapping his twin on the back, Vyroth stepped back. The second he did, the others who'd made the trip moved forward.

Tydrin greeted him first.

Wrapping him in a bear hug, his blood brother lifted him off the floor. Holding him, he jostled him, then set him down... hard. As the jolt jackhammered through his legs, Vyroth cupped the side of Tydrin's neck. He pulled, then pushed, rocking him back and forth. Dark purple eyes lit with happiness at the show of affection, his younger brother grinned. He smiled back and, thumping the side of his fist against his sibling's chest, turned toward Levin.

Eyes the color of glaciers collided with his. Ice dragon out in full force, artic air swirled, lowering the temperature in the room as the frosty SOB studied him. A quick scan. A quicker embrace, and Levin stepped back, giving Rannock a clear path.

"Motherfucker." With the brute force of a bronze dragon, Rannock slammed the flat of his hand into Vyroth's shoulder. He rocked sideways. Bruises left by Cyprus screamed in protest. Rubbing his arm, he frowned at Rannock. The bastard grinned back at him *"Wee whelp. You donnae look any worse for the wear."*

"Niki's doing."

Rannock glanced in her direction. *"She's pretty."*

"She has a sister," Tempel said, breaking into the conversation.

Dark brows popped skyward as Rannock absorbed the information. *"Where?"*

"America."

"Shite. Too far tae fly. Bad luck." Rannock said, devilry in his eyes.

Vyroth shook his head as happiness streamed through him. Finally. *Finally.* He stood alongside his brothers-in-arms, inside the circle of protection his pack provided. Months of wishing. Hours of hoping. Days spent dreaming of the moment he returned home and saw them again.

Turning his head, he held out his hand to Nicole. "Come here, *Tazleiah.* Meet my brothers."

"Braveheart?" Lips twitching, Cyprus gave him a look, razzing him about the endearment he'd given Nicole in Dragonese.

"Suits her," he said, watching his mate cross the room. Skirting a broken table leg, she rounded the couch and, giving his brothers-in-arms a wide berth, set her hand in his. He pulled her in close. As she bumped into his side, he wrapped his arm around her. He ran his gaze over her face. Better color. Less freaked out, but still strung tight. "All right, Niki?"

"You done fighting?"

Rannock snorted.

Vyroth ignored him. "Aye."

"Then I'm all right."

He huffed in amusement, then got down to business, introducing her to members of his pack. Wallaig and Kruger would come later. The males had no doubt drawn the short straws, making them the unlucky ones. None of his brothers-in-arms relished being left at home, but... a necessary sacrifice. Cyprus wanted two warriors protecting the lair at all times.

Pointing to each of his packmates, Vyroth ran through names and skills. Cyprus and Tydrin—fire dragons with fire-acid-lava combination exhales. Levin—ice dragon with a serious frosty side. Rannock —bronze dragon with a temperament so nasty, males, packmates included, refused to fight with him.

Nicole nodded as he explained, but didn't ask questions.

She was too busy staring at Cyprus.

Understandable.

He and his brother were identical. Same height. Same build. Same face. Exact replicas of each other with one notable difference. Cyprus's eyes were pale violet. Vyroth's were mismatched—one the same color as his twin's, the other electric blue.

Done staring at his twin, Nicole turned her gaze on him. "You realize every time you hit him, it's like hitting yourself, right?"

Levin chuckled.

Bronze-gold eyes sparking, Rannock shook his head.

Cyprus grinned at him, telling him without words Nicole passed muster. A relief. He liked the idea his twin accepted Nicole. Not that he needed approval. Energy-fuse didn't negotiate. The electrostatic current ruled by the Meridian acted instead, binding a warrior to his mate so tightly his life force entwined with hers, ensuring she lived a long, healthy life.

A bang echoed across the room.

Everyone turned to look at Tempel.

A bag of pancake mix in one hand, the male plunked a big bowl down on the countertop. "Who wants pancakes?"

"Me," Nicole said, bouncing on her toes. His lips curved. Happy about pancakes. Looking forward to breakfast. Over the drama. Completely adorable. So perfect for him hope filtered in, making the impossible—that she might love him one day—seem possible. "Is the griddle going?"

Tempel shook his head. "Your job, darlin'."

Heart in a tangle, Vyroth lifted his arm from around her shoulders.

With a smile, she bumped him with her hip and, nodding to his packmates, retraced her path through the debris. Staying where he stood, he watched her join Tempel in the kitchen.

Hellfire. The Goddess of all Things must love him.

No other explanation for the gift of Nicole.

Gaze glued to her, he watched her unearth a black griddle from inside a cupboard. As she set it on the stove and got to work, Vyroth rolled his shoulders. He needed to get ahold of himself. Re-establish his control before he left his brothers, picked up Nicole, and carried her back to bed.

A great idea, but not right now. With the sun set to go down in a couple of hours, stalling would hinder, not help the situation.

Telling his dragon half to behave, he refocused, grabbed cushions off the floor, threw the mess back onto the sectional, and sat down. His brothers-in-arms followed his lead, getting comfortable, kicking back as he began to explain.

Everything.

About Montgomery, the prison, and his imprisonment. About Nicole's role in his escape, Lapier's flash drive, the unreachable Belarus pack, and what he planned for the coming night. As he talked and the smell of cooking pancakes drifted, his brothers listened, asking questions, making suggestions, hashing out details, on board with the hunt... and killing the bastard responsible for taking his freedom.

25

W ind-drag jetting off his wing-tips, Vyroth came out of the clouds like a pissed-off archangel. Winter chill bit. He bit back, baring fangs as he rocketed over Cyprus. His twin treated him to a sharp look. Playing wingman to their commander, Levin and Tydrin raised scaly brows in question.

Ignoring the silent inquiry, Vyroth leveled out and focused on Tempel.

On point, ahead of the pack, his friend wasn't wasting time. Velocity set at spine-bending, he flew south, leaving the glow of city lights behind. Flat plains rolled into rocky terrain. Small trees angled into much larger ones, climbing up mountainsides. Powerful magic swirled in his friend's wake. Aggressive. Focused. Lethal. A blast of electrostatic current unique to Tempel.

The energy trail scored over his horns.

His scales tingled as each wave hit him and—

Thank the Goddess for earth dragons.

The warrior was a force of nature. Reading the planet's telemetry. Mining the topography. Following his nose as the earth talked to him, allowing him to chart a course.

Banking west, Tempel blasted over a rising mountain range.

Vyroth whipped around a jagged peak, matching with his friend's horn-torquing speed. Massive, spiraling spikes slashed through the air. He adjusted his trajectory, avoiding the lethal backlash of Tempel's tail, but didn't slow.

He needed to stay close.

The male knew where he was going.

Startling, but welcome news.

Without Tempel, he would've been shooting in the dark. Guessing with little to go on. Oh, he knew the general direction of Montgomery's lair. Could point west if standing in Stuttgart train station, but other than that bit of information? He had nothing. Couldn't say for sure where he'd been held or how to get back to the scene of Montgomery's crime.

Good thing Tempel wasn't confused.

The male might not have exact coordinates—the longs and lats—of the bastard's castle, but as the earth spoke to him, guiding him to the tunnel he dug out of the prison, the location narrowed, tightening the noose.

Diving over the snarling tip of the last peak, Vyroth followed as Tempel sped toward the edge of Black Forest. Dark treetops below. Bright moon obscured by wispy clouds above. A perfect night for flying, and by his estimation, little more than an hour away. Encouraging news, but...

He didn't like the set up.

Or the fact his mate rode in the helicopter with Rannock.

Checking her proximity, he tuned into Nicole's energy signal. Her aura flared, burning across his senses. Recalibrating his sonar, he gentled the imprint to get a read on her mood. Relaxed. Settled. Excited to be helping Rannock fly the helicopter—one hundred percent comfortable in the co-pilot seat, hammering his packmate with questions about the Hog.

Vyroth clenched his teeth.

The whole thing pissed him off. Not that he thought Rannock would hurt her. He trusted his brother-in-arms. The warrior would never touch a female who didn't belong to him, but...

Bloody hell.

Nicole shouldn't be sitting in the Hog at all.

She should be tucked safely inside the safehouse. Shielded by magic. Away from all danger. Not headed at breakneck speed toward a Dragonkind showdown.

Too bad he lost the argument.

His mate refused to be left behind. And fuck him, but... her reasons for coming along made sense.

First—the other women in Montgomery's lair would need her once rescued. No doubt traumatized, the females wouldn't trust a pack of strange males, fearing more mistreatment. Second—with the Belarus commander MIA, Tempel had no way of guaranteeing his pack wouldn't show up at the house. A slim possibility, but after hearing that news, Nicole put her foot down, becoming so stubborn Vyroth couldn't change her mind. And third—Cyprus (the bloody traitor) overrode his objections.

The commander of the Scottish pack wanted Nicole on standby.

She'd spent time inside of the castle. Had been held above stairs for a time. Been allowed to move through corridors and rooms, around staircases and multiple floors. She knew the layout. Could direct the hunt once he and his brothers tore through the castle's magical shield and broke inside.

Not that she'd be getting anywhere near Montgomery's lair.

Not tonight.

Never again.

Like it or not, Nicole would remain in the helicopter. Rannock would protect it, wrap an invisibility spell around the Hog, ensuring the enemy couldn't detect, never mind locate, the helicopter.

Terrific plan. In theory.

One worth championing, if his mate wasn't involved.

Wings spread wide, he shadowed Tempel as he slowed, moving from scale-rattling fast to smooth glide.

Scanning the terrain, Vyroth linked in. *"Tempel—how close?"*

"Five miles."

Two away from the three-mile marker. Once through the barrier, Montgomery and his crew would be able to detect him and his brothers-in-arms. The instant that happened, Vyroth lost the advantage. Montgomery would panic—do his best to bug out before the Scottish pack arrived. The bastard wasn't a warrior in the true sense of the word. He never met other males on equal footing, more interested in saving his own skin than fighting.

Focused on strategy, Vyroth fired up mind-speak. *"Cy—the play?"*

"Two fighting triangles. You, Tempel, and Tydrin fly in from the north." Cyprus said, assuming command. *"Levin, you're with me. We'll attack from the south, and Rannock—"*

"Half an hour behind you," Rotor chop battered the cosmic connection as Rannock joined in. *"I'll set the Hog down, make sure Niki's set, and meet you."*

Eyes on the forest, Vyroth scanned the terrain ahead. *"She doesnae leave the chopper, Ran."*

"Not a problem. She doesnae want tae be anywhere near the enemy lair." Rannock said, sounding convincing. *"She's on clean-up with the females afterward."*

Vyroth exhaled. Electricity puffed from his nostrils as relief rose hard. Thank the Goddess. Nicole was sticking to the plan. Going to stay put. Allow him to keep her safe while he went after Montgomery.

"Six warriors on his tail?" Dark purple scales flashed in his periphery as Tydrin rolled in, setting up shop on his wing-tip. *"The second Montgomery senses us, he'll pack it up and haul ass."*

"Gonna have tae close the gap quick," Levin said, frost icing in his voice.

"He's got multiple points of entry and egress."

"How many, Tempel?" he asked, as his friend dropped back to fly alongside him. Tydrin on one side, Tempel on the other. Kick-ass fighting triangle ready to inflict maximum damage.

"At this distance? I sense six, but... could be more." Glancing at him, Tempel nailed him with shimmering eyes. *"The asshole's smart."*

"You want a shot at him before I kill him?" Vyroth asked, feeling generous.

"Can you control yourself long enough to give me one?"

"Unlikely."

His brothers-in-arms chuckled.

Tempel grinned, baring fang. *"Do your worst, man. If there's anything left when I get there, I'll take my shot... for Niki."*

"For Niki." Thoughts of his mate—so beautiful, so

strong, so brave—whispered through his mind. Thoughts of revenge, of righting the wrong and giving her closure, followed. Aggression spiked, raising his hackles. *"And all the other females he's hurt."*

"Damn straight," his packmates growled at the same time.

"Quick and clean, lads. Make it brutal. Make it fast. Watch your arses." Orange wings spread wide, black white-flecked scales flashing, Cyprus banked south, breaking away from the group. *"See you on the flipside."*

The flipside.

After the battle.

After he'd killed Montgomery.

After the Scottish pack put an end to his cruelty along with his crew.

Justice, Dragonkind style. The way of his kind. Something each of his brothers-in-arms believed in and excelled at delivering. Increasing his wing speed, Vyroth cracked through the three-mile marker. His unique energy signal went live, broadcasting his position, giving Montgomery a heads-up as he flew in hot.

River water rumbled.

A waterfall cascaded over a high cliff. Mist billowed into the air, pebbling on—

"There," Tempel growled. *"See it?"*

Vyroth didn't answer.

Tucking his wings, he attacked, spiraling out of the sky. Seconds from hitting the shield protecting Montgomery's lair, he bared his fangs and exhaled. Toxic gas and lightning gathered in the back of his throat. He held the electrostatic pulse an instant, then unleashed hell.

Like a long-tailed comet, the ball of energy hammered the barrier.

Sparks flew.

Electricity roared.

The shield split, tearing wide open. Vyroth rocketed through the hole, hoping Montgomery wasn't as smart as Tempel claimed. Praying he dug in, stayed arrogant, and refused to run.

26

Standing in his room, Montgomery stood at the foot of his bed and stared. Hand-carved spiral posts twisted up from king-sized corners. Expensive damask curtains, tied back by fancy tassels, spilled onto the best mattress money could buy. Thick, soft, stylish comforter, silk sheets underneath. A horde of plush pillows leaning against a gilded headboard fit for a conqueror.

Luxurious.

Comfortable.

A love nest for the male he'd become.

Most females appreciated his room. Liked the decadence designed to show off the female form. Each curve. Every subtle shift of expression. Feminine wiles framed to perfection, bathed in candlelight, surrounded by dark colors and rich fabric as she danced for him.

Montgomery closed his eyes.

Dancing.

He always made them dance.

Selected his bedmates carefully, sometimes following a female for hours to observe how she moved, preferring lithe curves and graceful lines. Nicole would've been glorious dressed in the silk scarves he made his females wear.

Nothing but a pipe dream now.

He'd never get to watch her dance. Never get to teach her what he liked, how to move, or make her ride him while he watched her eyes turn smoky with desire.

Flexing his hands, he opened his eyes and growled low in his throat. Fucking Scot. Vyroth had ruined everything. *Everything*, and was about to fuck up the rest.

He knew the Scottish pack was on the move.

Not that he possessed any intel.

He was guessing more than anything else.

Vyroth was a warrior. A strong male, made stronger by warfare and a lifetime spent in the Highlands. The pack's reputation was well-established. Unforgiving. Brutal to the point of devastating. Lethal in all ways. No crime went unpunished under the Scottish commander's rule, so... yeah. The chances of Vyroth turning around and flying home existed somewhere between slim and none. Which meant...

Time to get out of Black Forest.

Before the Scottish pack laid siege to his fortress and he got trapped inside.

With a final glance at his bed, he turned toward the sitting area. Swiping the duffle bag off the couch, he strode toward the open door. Footfalls muffled by thick rugs, he stepped into the hallway and glanced at his first in command.

Slinging the bag over his shoulder, he tipped his chin. "All set?"

"Almost," Warsaw said, jogging toward him. "Rounding up the females now."

"The Numbai?"

"Out of commission."

Good.

Lapier deserved to die. The male had betrayed him, unlocking Nicole's cage, providing what she needed to help Vyroth escape. A low blow. A stupid move, given he'd rescued the male from the harsh reality of Rodin's lair. Had the Numbai proven loyal, Montgomery would've treated him like gold. Given him whatever he wanted to keep the lair running smoothly. Instead, the idiot had become attached to a female he didn't even know, putting Nicole above the good of his new pack.

Turning on his heels, he headed for the main staircase. Halfway down the hall, a tingle swept the nape of his neck. His sonar pinged. Montgomery reeled in the information. The three-mile marker squawked. Five unique energy signals appeared on his mental screen. Senses rocking, Montgomery shook his head.

Too soon.

Way too soon.

No way Vyroth should be in his airspace now. He thought he had hours to spare. Had left his hidey-hole in the mountains the instant the sun set, needing to be airborne and ahead of Vyroth before the male opened his eyes for the night.

"Shit," Warsaw growled. "Less than three minutes out."

Thinking fast, he mind-spoke to the males still inside the lair. *"Leave everything. Bug out, different exits, different directions."*

Affirmative replies came back as his pack obeyed his order.

"Let's go," he said to Warsaw, tossing the duffle. It hit the wall with a thud as he made tracks toward the end of the hall. Running hard, he hit the stairs at full tilt. Boots banging on stone treads, he unleashed magic. The hidden panel on the landing shifted out, then sideways, opening into an underground passageway.

Right on his heels, Warsaw sprinted into the tunnel. "Monty!"

"What?"

"The females. They're still upstairs. I didn't—"

"Leave them." His tiny dancers were Vyroth's problem now. In fact... revenge or the death of innocents. A perfect dilemma to toss in the Scot's lap. "Warsaw—light it up."

"The lair?"

He nodded. "Burn it. Burn it all."

His first in command hesitated.

And Montgomery understood. His friend had a soft spot for the fairer sex. He didn't care. Not right now. He and his warriors needed cover. Enough time to exit the lair, get airborne, and outfly Vyroth and the warriors with him. A fire—Warsaw's eternal flame— was the best and only solution to the problem.

Dragon half rising, venom bubbled in his veins.

He snarled at his first in command.

Warsaw lit the fuse. Heat detonated around him. Twin fireballs flared in the center of his friend's palms. Red-gold eyes glowing, Warsaw turned and hurled streams of flame into the stairwell. Fire exploded. The magic-fueled inferno roared, scorching stone, eating at wood, traveling down, going up, engulfing interior corridors.

Montgomery watched the blaze a moment, then turned and, with a murmur, closed the secret passageway, leaving Lapier and the females to burn.

27

Curled up in the co-pilot's seat, Nicole stared out the cockpit window. Thick glass between her and the outside world. Dense woods, branches spread wide, stood across the clearing. A safe place. A place far from the castle. The place Rannock set the helicopter down. A quiet cove surrounded by forest, burnished by moonlight and solemn night sounds.

The chirp of insect songs unsettled her.

Creaking trees made her tense.

Somehow, nature's music sounded ominous. Like a warning in the dark. As though the chorus of crickets knew something she didn't about where she sat—that danger lurked around the edges, in the shadows, maligning the clearing, scoffing at the spot the guys believed was safe.

A trick of the imagination, no doubt.

The summoning of ghosts that didn't exist and never would.

The idea should've comforted her. Settled and encouraged her. Making sure she stayed out of the way until needed was the objective. Vyroth didn't want her anywhere near the fighting.

Nicole agreed, but...

She shifted in her seat. Waiting wasn't her strong suit. She didn't like the stillness. Couldn't keep from fidgeting. Kept imagining what she'd do if the bogeyman showed up.

Surrounded by buttons and dials, Nicole wrapped her arms around her knees. Attention on the forest, she looked for movement in the trees. Nothing. All quiet on the screwed-up front. She should be happy about that—ready to stand up and cheer. Getting anywhere near the castle wasn't a good idea. Her mind shied every time she thought about going back, shielding her from what happened to her there.

Her heart, however?

Her heart wasn't invested in safety. It wanted to be out there in the thick of it, making her think about all the things she ought to be doing. The longer she sat alone in the dark, the longer the list grew. She should be playing a part—providing intel about the castle layout, describing the women trapped inside, reminding Vyroth about Lapier. Helping with the mission instead of sitting on her duff miles from the frontline.

The designated stand-by position made her feel like a coward. Weak. Less than. Unable to contribute to the new life she wanted to build with Vyroth. Which was ridiculous... and she knew it.

Logic pointed out all the pertinent facts.

She was human, not Dragonkind. Believing she could move the dial (even a little) in a dragon battle leaned away from common sense, jetting straight into stupidity. And yet, her mind churned, keeping a running tally of *should-be-doings*. And surprise, surprise, twiddling her thumbs inside a helicopter, surrounded by an invisibility shield, waiting for the guys to give the all clear, didn't appear anywhere on the list.

Worry wort gene in fine form, she stewed about all the bad things that could be—

Snick.

Creak.

Thud.

Nicole tensed, sitting up straighter in her seat. Her focus sharpened on the woods.

A shadow zigzagged between tree trunks. The man was moving at a steady click, looking over his shoulder. Leaves rustled above his head. Pine boughs dipped and swayed, shedding needles. Time slowed as the stranger stepped out of the murk into the clearing.

Gaze glued to him, Nicole slid her feet off the seat onto the floor.

Still looking over his shoulder, the guy transformed into a red dragon. Cold air displaced. Fog swirled along the ground as he flexed his wings. Flames flickering off the tips of twisted brown horns, he looked skyward.

Nicole swallowed. Crap. Sometimes she hated being right, 'cause...

The bogeyman existed.

The beast stood in her line of sight, less than fifty feet away.

"Go, go, go," she breathed, afraid to move. "Fly away. Fly away."

He opened his wings.

A gust of wind rushed across the clearing, broadsiding the helicopter. Metal shuddered as the steel body rocked on rubber tires.

Shimmering dark eyes snapped in her direction.

Pressed into the seatback, Nicole quivered. "Don't move. He can't see you, he can't see you, he can't see you."

The dragon's gaze narrowed. He scanned the clearing.

Another wind gust battered the helicopter.

His nostrils flared.

Fire rippling along his spiked spine, he hissed and, jagged tail snaking out behind him, walked in her direction. Massive paws flattened the long grass. Watching him approach, Nicole fought the urge to scramble, trying to think. What should she do? Moving wasn't a good idea. Rannock had given her strict instructions—stay in the cockpit, don't leave the helicopter, stay as still as possible. The invisibility spell surrounding her counted on low energy. Minimal displacement. Was design to shield inanimate objects, so...

"Shit."

Being high-energy sucked. At least, right now. When she and Vyroth connected, the sizzle blew her mind, but here, staring down the snout of an enemy dragon? Not so much.

Panic circling, Nicole tried to decide. Move or not? Trust the spell or make a break for it? Good questions. Ones she couldn't answer as the red dragon prowled closer. Almost on top of her, he scented the air. Hot dragon breath rolled over the glass. Scaly brows furrowed, he stared right through her, trying to figure out what bothered him. A growl rippled as he lifted a paw, talons outstretched, claws less than a foot away and—

A dark orange blur slammed into him.

The red dragon roared as his body torqued.

Tangled up, claws flashing, tails whipping, the dragons tumbled across the turf. Chunks of grass flew into the air. Dirt rained down, showering the helicopter, pinging off steel. Bronze shimmer washed into the cockpit, glinting off the second dragon's metallic scales. Shielding her eyes, Nicole stared as the bronze dragon grabbed the bad guy's horns.

He twisted.

Bones snapped.

Blood spilled onto the ground.

Tongue hanging out of his mouth, the red dragon slumped. Talons buried in his opponent's throat, the bronze dragon dug deeper, sinking his claws in until the dragon he pressed into the long grass disintegrated.

Grey ash spilled into the wind, blowing up and over the cockpit.

Metallic scales gleaming, the victor met her gaze through the windshield. "Get out."

Nicole blinked. "Rannock?"

He bared huge fangs. "Move yer arse, Niki."

"But..." She shuffled around the pilot chair. "I'm supposed to stay put."

"Cannae leave you here. Not now," he said, shaking ash out of his claws. "You're bleeding energy. The invisibility shield cannae contain it all, so yer coming with me."

Lovely. Just terrific.

She knew the whole high-energy thing would get her in trouble. "Sorry."

"I donnae want yer apology. I want you moving."

"What about—"

"Fuck," he barked, glaring at her. "HE females—total pains in the arse. Get out... now."

Well. All right then.

Obviously, not the time to argue. Or ask for an explanation.

Leaving the cockpit, Nicole hustled into the back of the chopper. She scrambled down the center aisle, past wide leather seats to the door. A second before she grabbed the handle, it turned. The door folded out. She raced down the steps. Rannock stalked around the front of the helicopter and, reaching out with a massive paw, plucked her off the ground.

She landed on his back with a thump.

"Hold on, Niki."

Her hands found the spikes behind his horns. "Is Vyroth all right? Is everything—"

"It's all gone tae shite." Unfolding his wings, Rannock leapt skyward. Bitter cold blasted over her a second before warm air close around her. "Total clusterfuck."

Fear tightened her chest.

She breathed through it, but... his answer didn't inspire confidence. Or help tamp down her fear.

Hanging on tight, Nicole leaned into the flight, praying Vyroth was all right. Safe. Unhurt. Able to defend and attack.

She didn't care about Montgomery. Or what happened inside his lair.

Not anymore.

All that mattered was Vyroth.

She needed him. Much more than she needed to be avenged. Righting the wrong wouldn't change what happened. Nothing would, but she'd heal. Vyroth was already helping her—keeping her safe, calming her nerves, connecting with her in ways she didn't yet understand but knew made all the difference. With Vyroth in her corner, she'd battle the monster and come out a winner.

But only if he came back to her.

"Rannock," she whispered as he rocketed across the night sky, over treetops toward a distant river.

"Not now, lass."

She didn't want to wait. She wanted to ask—to

pepper him with questions and find out what was happening—but shut down the impulse.

Rannock's reaction told her everything she needed to know.

He didn't have time to explain... or reassure. He needed to reach his packmates, before bad became worse, and Vyroth (or one of his brothers) ended up dead.

28

Cloaked in magic, Vyroth tore another hole in the invisibility shield surrounding Montgomery's lair. Shards of energy raked his side, screeching over his scales. Sparks flashed in his wake. Ignoring the fireworks, he spiraled through the gap, clearing the jagged edges left by his exhale. Ready for attack, he flipped one way, then opened his wings and banked hard in the other direction

Taut muscles pulled, stretching as he searched for enemy dragons and eyed what remained. Despite tears in the shield, the spell held firm, obscuring the castle and outbuildings. Which didn't work for him.

He needed to decimate the spell.

Rip it apart and dismantle the magic.

Punching a couple of holes in it wasn't good enough.

With most of the invisibility spell intact, Montgomery and his warriors could still use it for cover. The bastard was no doubt already on the move, using the remaining magic to interfere with Vyroth's ability to track his flight from castle. So aye. The shield needed to come down. All the way. He wanted a clear line of sight. Needed to be able to find and follow the cosmic trail the enemy pack left in its wake.

Head on a swivel, he searched the invisibility shield, looking for more points of weakness. He spotted it on the other side of the castle. Exhaling hard, Vyroth unleashed another energy ball. Electrostatic pulse shot between his fangs. Lightning streamed over the ancient walls, slamming into the shield. Blue light flickered, undulating like a wave, revealing the magical structure of the spell.

Tucking his wings, Vyroth flipped sideways.

Up and over. Around one of the turrets. Eyes narrowed on the prize.

He hammered the shield with another blow. Electrical charge tore through the enchantment. The spell flexed, held a second, then disintegrated, exposing the castle to night air and unseeing eyes.

Wheeling into a turn, he scanned the setup.

Hewn from solid rock, sitting on top of a cliff, the fortress reached for the sky. Four stories. Narrow windows. Thick walls. A wide cobblestoned courtyard on the north side. A tumbling river rushing passed on the west side. Angry water crashed around the foundation, throwing mist, making the castle appear as dark as the forest surrounding it.

Figured.

A lair the same color as the bastard's heart—the blackest of black.

"I'm inside," he mind-spoke to his brothers.

Out of range, south of the sprawling complex, Cyprus hit him up for more intel. *"Shield?"*

"Down. Clear line of sight."

"Anything?"

"Nothing yet. The castle's huge. Buildings on both sides of the river."

Night vision pinpoint sharp, Vyroth circled around the west side, looking for the unique energy signal Montgomery threw off like confetti. He scanned the outbuildings. He searched the cliffside and bluffs. His gaze tracked over the bridge, along the river and both shorelines.

Nothing.

No trace energy in the air.

Nothing to suggest the enemy was escaping from hidden tunnels.

Flying over the river, he swooped under the bridge. The river roared below him. Water pebbled his scales as he slowed to a glide above the castle. Shaped like a diamond, the structure sprawled, taking up the entire clifftop. Eyes trained on the main structure, he hunted along the parapet, searching towers and the outer bailey.

Something flickered in his periphery.

The smell of smoke hit him. His gaze snapped left and—

"*Shite.*" Wings spread wide, Vyroth put on the brakes. Hanging in mid-air, he looked through a narrow window. Orange tendrils flickered behind the frame—fast moving, wave-like, growing into a monster. "*Fire.*"

"*I see it.*" Dark purple scales flashing, Tydrin streaked overhead. "*I'm going inside. See if I can—bloody hell. Not good.*"

Circling overhead, he watched his brother fly in low. "*What?*"

"*The bastard lit the fuse with eternal flame.*"

"*Any way tae put it out?*"

"*I can slow it down, but...*" Flames rippling along his spiked spine, Tydrin landed on the roof. His claws clicked against stone. Perched on the rampart, he shook his head. *"Eternal flame cannae be extinguished. The fire'll burn until it has nothing left tae eat."*

"The asshole. Told you he was smart." Streaking beneath him, Tempel turned hard and came up fast, flipping over his wing-tip. *"There are people inside."*

"You sure?" Shifting to human form, Tydrin headed for a door in one of the corner turrets.

"Three aboveground, in the castle. Two females, one male."

Vyroth clenched his teeth. The bastard. The fire was nothing but a tactic. One designed to slow him down. *"The prison?"*

"Empty," Tempel said, reading dirt and stone, picking details out of the earth.

"Are the females mobile?" Yanking the door open, Tydrin disappeared inside. *"Injured?"*

"No, but... goddamn the asshole." Baring fang, Tempel growled. *"They don't stand a chance. He locked them in."*

"Electrified cages?" Vyroth asked, wanting to know if he needed to land.

"Maximum wattage, man."

Fire hissing around him, Tydrin cursed.

"Tydrin—slow the fire," he said, frustration burning through him. He didn't want to land. Not with Montgomery in open air and the hunt alive in his veins. He needed to kill the male more than he wanted his next breath, but... hellfire. He couldn't leave innocents to burn. Refused to be that male—so caught up in his own wants he ignored the needs of others. *"Tempel—what floors?"*

"First floor."

"All three?"

"Same room," Tempel said, feeding him the necessary information. *"Southeast corner."*

Whirling into another turn, Vyroth set up his approach. The roof wouldn't work. He needed somewhere else to land. Somewhere with enough space for him in dragon form. Somewhere close to the southeast corner of the castle. A place he wouldn't have to fight through an inferno to reach the captives. Gaze locked on the ground, he made another pass and—

The large courtyard came into view.

Folding his wings, Vyroth dropped out of the sky. Winter air whistled off the tips of his horns. Water rolled off his spiked spine, spiraling in the rush. His paws slammed down on cobblestone. Wide pavers cracked beneath his claws a moment before he shifted, moving from dragon to human form.

Fire roared against interior windowpanes.

Glass melted. Burning chunks of wood rained down.

Dodging hot embers, he sprinted toward the stairs. Taking the treads three at a time, he snarled a command. Magic whiplashed. Heavy double doors blew inward, tearing off ancient hinges. Avoiding the tumbling wood panels, he raced into what looked like a great hall.

Thick smoke.

Waves of oxygen-stealing heat.

The glow of fire, but no flames in the main room yet.

"Through the front door." Leaping over a flight of stairs, Vyroth sprinted past a couch, vaulted over a chair, and ran into a corridor on the other side of the room. *"Cyprus—"*

"Five miles away." A vicious snarl rolled through mind-speak. *"Change of plan, lads."*

"Cy," he growled in warning.

"No other play, brother. You're the only one who can

open the cages." Wind-rush blew through the link as Cyprus changed direction. *"Get those trapped inside out. Levin and I will hunt. Pick up Montgomery's trail and—"*

"He's mine, brother."

Cyprus huffed. *"We'll bring him tae ground. After I question him, he's all yours."*

Vyroth growled.

He despised the new plan. Didn't like what it meant or that his twin would have first crack at Montgomery, but... shite. Cyprus was right. Battle plans needed to be fluid during a hunt. Strategy was always subject to circumstance and change. A skilled warrior allowed for flexibility. Could accept a new direction on the fly, learned to adjust when things didn't go his way.

Like now.

Montgomery was long gone. Nowhere near the lair. Already in full flight. His ability to map a male's signature provided the intel. Lack of trace energy did the rest. The absence in the air, the lack of a cosmic trail, told no lies.

The male had lit the fuse and fled, taking valuable prisoners, leaving inconsequential ones behind. Brutal decision. Cruel beyond measure. Most thought drowning was the worst way to die and, given his aversion to water, Vyroth agreed. But honestly, burning to death had to be a close second.

Rounding a blind corner, Vyroth dodged as hot embers rained down. Eating through wood, a wall of flames rolled along the heavy beamed ceiling, undulating like a wave overhead. Choking on smoke, he got low and kept moving. Jumping over a burning beam, he searched both sides of the southeast corridor. Staggered along the hall, doors marched down both sides and—

Static electricity hit him.

The fine hairs on his nape rose.

Eyes narrowed, he tracked the fluctuating current and... *there*. Last door, left-hand side.

Hopscotching across burning floorboards, Vyroth unlocked the door with a mental command. He pushed it open with his mind. An instant later, he crossed the threshold. Fire followed him, leaping from door jamb to floor, crawling across the wooden planks, reaching for the area rug. Hellish heat rolled in behind him. Thick smoke followed, billowing into the room, obscuring his vision as he hunted for the zip of electricity.

Hard current crackled to his right.

Whipping soot off his face, he let his dragon half lead. Lightning sparked in his palms. Harnessing the power, he moved toward the—

Harsh coughing sounded.

A soft sob followed.

Three cages materialized out of the smoke.

"Found'em. Tempel—make me a hole."

A blast of magic rammed the castle. The outer wall cracked. Ancient stone shook, then whiplashed, exploding outward, toward the river.

Fresh air blew in through the hole.

A dark shadow with glowing eyes appeared in the void.

Grabbing hold of the steel bars, Vyroth unleashed his magic. Electricity arched. High voltage cracked overhead. Lightning bolts arching from his hands, he absorbed the current, overloading the system, blowing electrical circuits all over the castle.

The locking mechanism clicked.

Wrenching the door open, he went after the first female. Nothing but a rag doll. Barely conscious. Fighting for each breath.

Working fast, he hauled her out of the cage and tossed her in Tempel's direction. One down. He moved to the next and repeated the process, throwing her toward the hole in the wall. Claws clicked as Tempel caught both and pushed away from the castle wall. Freefalling, he unfolded his wings and disappeared into the gloom.

Vyroth moved to the last cage. Male down. No movement. Grabbing his ankles, he dragged him out and... smelled the blood. His attention jumped to the Numbai's face. A deep wound on the side of his head, the male lay on his side, still alive, but...

He wouldn't remain that way. Not without a serious amount of medical attention.

"Fuck," Vyroth snarled as he slung the male over his shoulder. *"Tydrin—how much time?"*

"Propane tanks in the basement. The place is going tae blow," Tydrin said, breathing hard, the sound of pounding feet coming through mind-speak. *"Get out, brother. Get out n—"*

The inferno hissed behind him.

A fireball exploded in through the open door.

Hot fingers lashed the backs of his legs as Vyroth ramped into a run.

He lunged toward the side wall. Dead weight, the Numbai listed to one side, taking him off balance as an explosion rocked the room. Steel cages shattered. Shrapnel blasted into the room. Pain ripped through his side as the shock wave blew him straight through the stone wall, hurling him toward the rocks below.

29

Stunned by the collision, Vyroth free-fell into open air. Wind whipped past his head, but time slowed. His ears rang, but he didn't hear the clamor. Unable to figure out where he was, Vyroth shook his head. Instinct roared, urging him to move, adjust, figure out who kept shouting his name.

Twisted by the mental fog, voices distorted, sounding far away, hissing through mind-speak. Multiple males yelling. The violent sound of wings flapping. The clutch and scrawl of urgent messages he couldn't understand.

Feeling scrambled, he tightened his hold on the male he held. He blinked rapid-fire, the smell of blood in his nose, smoke coiled in his lungs, trying to get his bearings.

Spinning in space.

Falling through wet murk.

Lots of wind. Lots of noise. In human form.

The realization jolted through him. His brain came back online. The sky above him cleared. Tendrils of flame roared out a hole in the wall above him. Mist everywhere. The crashing rumble of a river at his back. A female screaming. A male yelling for him to shift.

Good idea.

The best given he was falling.

Plugging into his magic, Vyroth transformed into dragon form. Blue-black scales replaced his skin. His wings unfolded. The webbing caught air. Brutal torque stretched sore muscles. Agony stabbed him in the ribs, then swung around to hammer his lower back. Grimacing, cradling the male in his talons, he flipped upright.

The snarl of jagged rocks rose to greet him.

He cursed and, gritting his teeth, put on the brakes, moving from fast plummet to painful hover. Unsteady, he wobbled in mid-air, see-sawing above the rapids. Frothing, snarling over huge rocks, cold water tumbled over his tail. Pulling himself free, he flapped his wings, lifting his bulk away from the river rush.

Wings angled, he whirled around the lower cliffs.

The waterfall came into view.

He flew toward it, then went vertical, rocketing straight up the wall of water. Dipping beneath the bridge, he shot skyward into open sky and looked around.

The castle and complex below him. The vastness of an ancient forest stretched in front him. A dark orange blur streaked across the sky.

Energy raked across his senses.

He locked on and... hellfire. The male had lost his mind. What the hell did Rannock think he was doing?

"Ran," he snarled, focused on Nicole and where she sat on his packmate's back. *"I'm going tae kill you."*

"Couldn't leave her there, lad," Rannock said, com-

pletely unconcerned by his threat. *"She was a sitting duck in the Hog... leaking energy all over the place."*

His brows collided.

Sucked, but... a reasonable explanation.

Vyroth ground his back molars together. So much for beating the shite out of his friend. Much as it pained him, Rannock was right. Nicole should never have been left alone in the chopper. He hadn't like it then, didn't like it now. Should've known better—realized an invisibility spell was no match for an HE female.

Plugged into the Meridian, Nicole's energy was too potent for standard Dragonkind tricks. She required more than simple camouflage. She needed powerful magic to shield her, the kind he supplied while touching her. Without him to draw off the excess energy, her signal burned bright, making her vulnerable, ensuring she remained a high-value target in his world.

Energy like hers attracted attention.

All kinds of it. Most of it unwanted.

Once locked onto the beacon, warriors would drop everything to hunt for a female as powerful as Nicole... and fight to keep her, once found.

Vyroth blew out a breath. Electricity sparked in his exhale as he shook his horned head. He needed to stop stalling. Quit avoiding *'the talk'* Tempel wanted him to have with her. The last thing he wanted to do was scare his mate, but given Rannock's news, little choice remained. He wanted Nicole safe—undetectable by Montgomery, unencumbered by stress, able to live a worry-free life. Which left one option—explain energy regression, how altering her energy worked, and what it meant for her—for him—going forward.

Eternal energy-fuse.

Matehood.

Complete commitment to one another.

He longed for it. Yearned to make her his forever, but rushing Nicole wouldn't work. His female must make up her own mind. Choose to stay with him without fear driving her decision.

"Here—trade." Flying in close, Rannock set up shop next to him. He held out a massive paw, then flicked his black metallic claws, making a gimme gesture. *"Toss me the male. You take her."*

A welcome trade. An offer he wouldn't refuse. *"Gently, Ran. He's in bad shape."*

"Knock tae the noggin?"

"Aye," Rolling into a smooth glide, he stabilized his flight. Jarring the Numbai wasn't a good idea. He might be breathing, but too quick a shift could kill him. Movements slow, he laid him in his friend's outstretched paw.

"Still breathing." Cradling the injured male, using a gentle touch, Rannock turned the Numbai's head. Bronze gaze on the side of his head, his packmate examined the wound. *"Bleeding's stopped. Good sign."*

"Is Lapier all right?" Worry in her eyes, small hand wrapped around one of Rannock's spikes, Nicole leaned sideways. The instant her gaze landed on the Numbai, her face paled. "Is he dead? Vyroth, is he—"

"Nay, *Tazleiah*." Reaching out, Vyroth plucked her off his brother-in-arm's back. She barely noticed. Busy staring at the male who'd helped her escape, she accepted the shift in position without comment. "Unconscious."

"He needs help. A doctor. Is there a hospital nearby?"

Rannock snorted. "Have you gone mad, lass? He's

Numbai, not human. Yer doctors'll shite their pants if we take him tae one of yer hospitals."

"Then what—"

"Hold on, Niki," Banking south, Vyroth fired up mind-speak. *Everybody check in—update.*"

"*Flying into a nearby town,*" Tydrin said, static hissing through the connection. "*Got Tempel with me.*"

"*The females?*"

"*Freaked out, but still breathing. Gonna set them down outside the ER. Both need to be checked out. Once we—*"

"*Fucking hell. You sure, Levin?*" Crashing the conversation, Cyprus voice burst through mind-speak, his tone so intense Rannock flinched.

Vyroth tensed. "*Status?*"

"*Dead air,*" Cyprus snarled. "*We got less than nothing. No trace. No trail tae follow. The bastard slipped through our net.*"

"*Goddamn it.*" Vyroth flexed his talons. Would nothing go right tonight?

"*Total goatfuck, lads,*" Rannock said, flying off his right wing-tip. "*Time tae rethink.*"

The pronouncement spiraled through the link.

Static came over the line.

Total silence. The magical equivalent of a Dragonkind temper tantrum.

Vyroth almost laughed. *Almost,* but not quite.

Under normal circumstances, he would've found his brother-in-arm's reaction to Rannock's suggestion funny. It was, after all, noteworthy. The Scottish pack never went silent. Stubborn to the core, the lethal males believed in communication—the more provoking, the more offensive, the better. But with Montgomery and his crew flying away scot-free, Vyroth shared his packmate's aversion.

None of the warriors wanted to abandon the hunt.

Each one wanted to find and kill Montgomery as much as he did.

But as the silence stretched on—and on—Vyroth felt the weight. Cyprus would hunt until the sun forced him to stop. His brothers would follow his twin's lead, which meant... he must be the one to break the stalemate. To start talking sense. To fall-back to a reasonable position in light of new information.

"I donnae like it any more than you do, but..." He trailed off, laminating the burden of leadership. Disappointment reared its ugly head, spiraling deep. Vyroth shoved it aside. He refused to chase shadows. Someone must lead by example—with his head, not his heart. *"We got fuck-all tae go on. I'm calling it."*

Cursing blazed through mind-speak as his packmates sounded off.

"You sure, V?" Cyprus asked, prepared to beat the bushes all night if it meant unearthing Montgomery. *"We've got a couple of hours until daybreak."*

"Hunting blind, Cy. Waste of time." He shook his head, then looked over his shoulder. He met his female's gaze. Read the concern in her eyes. Felt her hands stroke over his scales, smoothing away frustration, soothing him with her touch. Hellfire. His female. Generous to a fault. Beautiful in her affection. A true treasure. One he didn't deserve to keep if he refused to shift course and put her first. *"No more tonight. I've got my mate tae protect. Niki's more important than that bastard."*

"We'll get'im," Tydrin said, trying to make him feel better. *"Eventually."*

"I'll put out feelers," Levin said, his tone shiver inducing. *"Collect intel. Track the bastard. Find the patterns —where he's been, what he likes, who he knows, the places*

he frequents. Get a complete picture, so when the time comes, we can turn the screws."

God bless the cold nature of ice dragons.

Levin was the king of covert operations. Skilled in the art of negotiation. Frighteningly thorough when conducting interrogations. So stealthy that experienced warriors never realized they'd caught Levin's attention until far too late.

"Sounds like a plan, Lev," he said, appreciating his packmate's offer.

Frustrated, but resigned, Cyprus growled. *"Rendezvous at the Hog. Minsk, then home, lads."*

Minsk.

Home to the Belarusian warrior pack. One in constant disaccord with Rodin and the Russian enclave. From what Tempel explained, the feud had lasted years. Battles over territory. Disputes over sovereignty. Too many males left dead over centuries. An area most warriors avoided unless given express permission to visit, but...

Tempel needed answers.

The mystery of his silent pack needed to be solved.

Vyroth refused to let him go alone. Which naturally led to his brothers-in-arms volunteering to make the trip with him. A welcome offer, given he didn't know what awaited Tempel in Minsk. Missed phone calls one day didn't signal disaster. Given his friend's level of concern, however, the radio silence didn't inspire confidence either.

Instinct was a useful thing.

Vyroth's was well-honed. And his was pinging, warning him something was off in Belarus. The kind of wrong that would not only upend Tempel, but send shockwaves through the rest of Dragonkind.

30

Snuggled up in Vyroth's lap, Nicole listened to the thump of helicopter rotors and watched dark ripples keep sunlight from penetrating the small window opposite her. Strange juxtaposition. Human-designed helicopter, Dragonkind magic co-existing in perfect harmony. The contrast and compare elements were striking. Full daylight outside, zero sunlight inside a tricked-out military machine. Blackout conditions but for the soft glow of strip lights embedded in the carpeted floor.

Her attention drifted across the center aisle.

Her lips twitched.

Never let it be said Vyroth and his cohorts didn't know how to kick back.

Sprawled out, seatbacks reclined all the way, Cyprus and Levin slept despite the noise and shimmy of the helicopter. Tempel sat up front with Rannock, directing the flight, helping him navigate. Though how either of them could see with the cockpit glass blacked out Nicole didn't know.

Sophisticated radar equipment, maybe.

Dragon sonar, probably.

Practice at avoiding deadly UV rays while mobile during the day, without a doubt.

Closing her eyes, Nicole tried to follow the guys' lead. Lie back. Relax. Get some sleep while she had the chance. Vyroth warned her she needed the rest, but... she sighed. Every time she tried to doze off, her brain kicked over. Now, her mind raced, throwing out all kinds of interesting thoughts.

Drawing the blanket over her shoulder, Nicole nestled deeper into Vyroth. He purred. His arms tightened, drawing her closer. Warm, snug, cheek pressed to his shoulder, she listened to him breathe. Steady rise and fall of his chest. Strong thump of his heartbeat. Fast asleep in the seat he shared with her.

Something about the cozy arrangement settled her.

An odd kind of miracle.

Who knew being kidnapped would lead her here —to him, the man-dragon of her dreams.

Her sister would stick a label on it. Call her collision with Vyroth fate, the all-knowing universe at work. A cosmic thread woven together within the framework of wrong place, right time.

Habit and long-held beliefs wanted Nicole to disagree. Problem was... she couldn't. As starry-eyed as Cate could sometimes be, the weird turn of events fit the pattern. Smacked of more than serendipity and good fortune. There was rhyme. There was reason. And as she sat quietly, surrounded by Dragonkind guys, on her way to meet more, Nicole admitted her sister might be onto something.

Maybe Cate wasn't a crazy romantic.

Maybe (*just maybe*) she'd had it right all along.

Maybe the universe had penciled Vyroth into her

star chart, mapping out the arc of her life, choosing now to execute.

Vyroth shifted beneath her. "Heavy thoughts, *Tazleiah.*"

"A little. Someone's gotta tackle the world's problems."

"And that's you?"

She shrugged. "Today? Maybe."

"Thinking about us?"

"Yeah. Crazy as it is, I've been wandering through life. Rootless. Lost. Searching for something," she whispered, thinking about her dad and the way he lived. Moving around, jumping from one thing to another, searching for 'the good life.' Which for him meant *easy.* "All this time, and I just realized—I've been looking for you all along."

"Niki," he murmured, the yearning in his voice so thick it burrowed into her heart.

"Do you believe in fate, Vyroth?"

"I believe in magic. Matched mates and the undeniability of cosmic connection."

"No need to qualify it?" she asked, tracing the heavy metal logo on his T-shirt. "No need to explain?"

"Not even a wee bit."

A romantic. A believer, like Cate. "Force of nature."

"Once unleashed, impossible to stop."

Laying her palm over his heart, she glanced up at him. Slumped in the seat, head tipped back, he stared at her from beneath the fan of his dark lashes. His mismatched eyes flashed, pale purple and electric blue—an arresting combination. Unable to resist, she stroked his beard. Played in the rough whiskers. Reveled in the feel of him, trying to ground herself, struggling to understand her quick-silver reaction. How had it happened so fast? Why did merely meeting Vyroth mean falling for him?

No grace period.

No chance to adjust.

Zero to love at first sight, in sixty seconds flat.

Trailing her fingertip over his eyebrow, she kissed the side of his throat. "Tell me it's real, honey. I'm down the rabbit hole, falling hard."

"I'm right here, lass. I've already caught you."

She smiled.

Of course he had.

Every time she needed him to, he answered the call, reassuring her, helping her understand, providing information without her asking. The strength of the connection she shared with him ought to scare her. At first, it had. She'd tried to block out the truth—the vibration, the buzz in her veins, her ability to sense his mind. But as her fingers whispered over his cheekbone, she relaxed into the sensation, realizing what the hum signified—the magical side of him reaching out for her. Wanting to connect. Needing to feel her. Longing to be accepted in the same way she yearned to belong.

The thought, like so many others, nudged her toward an unescapable realization.

She loved him.

Had the fall been fast? Yes. Could she deny what he made her feel? No. Which meant...

She needed to tell him.

Now. Before logic grabbed hold, reason reengaged, and she lost all courage.

"Vyroth, I—"

"Look alive, sports fans," Rannock said from the cockpit. Rotors thumping, the helicopter swung into a wide turn. Her stomach dipped as the frame shuddered, then plunged into rapid descent. "Dropping into the pit."

"Hellfire." Raising his head, Vyroth glared at the front of the helicopter. "Bad timing, Ran."

"Have yer lovefest later, V." Blackout glass rippled as, hands and feet at the controls, Rannock looked over his shoulder. His bronze gaze lit with humor, he winked at her. "Quit distracting him, Niki. We're descending into a vertical cave. Looks good, but we need his mind sharp, not full of mush."

Vyroth mumbled something nasty under his breath.

Nicole clenched her teeth, trying not to laugh.

"Not funny, lass."

"Beg to differ, honey," she said as he sat up, taking her with him.

"Oh, you'll be begging." Dipping his head, he nipped her bottom lip. "Later... when I get you alone."

Delicious threat full of carnal heat.

More of the intense pleasure he delivered at the safehouse.

Nicole shivered in delight. Vyroth kissed her hard, then shifted focus. Attention on Rannock, he stood, set her in his seat, and walked toward the cockpit. Her gaze darted across aisle and—

"Well met, lass." The devil in his eyes, Cyprus grinned at her. "Makes me yearn for home and my own female."

"Lord help me," she muttered, not knowing whether to be embarrassed or proud of Vyroth's obvious desire for her.

"Proud, lass," Levin said, mischief in his tone. "Definitely proud."

She frowned at him. "Get out of my brain, Levin."

He chuckled.

Noise battered the helicopter.

The descent slowed.

Oval windows began to lighten, moving from black to shades of pale grey.

Turning in her seat, Nicole pressed her face close to the window. Shadows sifted beyond the glass. Sunlight faded as the Hog descended further into the hole. Parts of the glass cleared. A jagged rock wall came into view.

The helicopter's rubber tires bumped down.

Pressing a bunch of buttons, Rannock shut the engines down.

Watching Cyprus and Levin move to the door, Nicole left her seat to check on Lapier. Lying on a gurney at the rear of helicopter next to the bathroom. Covered in thick blankets. Gauze wrapped around his head. IV plugged into one of his arms. Still unconscious, but...

She pressed her fingers to his pulse point. And breathed out in relief. Strong heartbeat, breathing steady, a little more color in his cheeks. Chewing on the inside of her lip, she fussed with his blankets, tugging the thick wool under his chin.

"Niki."

With a gentle hand, she touched Lapier's cheek, then looked over her shoulder.

"He stays in the chopper." Standing in the open door, Vyroth held out his hand. "Too dangerous tae move him."

"He'll be safe here? I can stay. I can—"

He shook his head. "Learned my lesson. Where I go, you go, until I get you home. Behind the powerful magic that protects our lair. Come here, *Tazleigh*."

With a nod, she obeyed. No one wanted a repeat of what happened in the clearing. Staying with Lapier would no doubt put him in more danger than if left to recover on his own.

Taking his hand, she followed Vyroth out of the helicopter, across uneven rocky ground, toward a tunnel cut into the sidewall. Just before she entered, she looked up. Vertical cave was right. Cut into the earth, smooth walls with spiral groves corkscrewed down from the surface. Tufts of distant trees hung over the edge. Nothing but a round pinprick of light at the top.

With a tug, Vyroth drew her into the tunnel.

Odd-looking lanterns bobbed against the ceiling like jellyfish, powered by... Nicole frowned. Nothing— no wires or electrical outlets, but glowing just the same, banishing the darkness as Tempel led the group down the underground passage.

"Magic," she whispered, enchanted by the floating lanterns.

"It's everywhere," Vyroth murmured back. "All you need do is look."

"And believe."

"Aye, that too." He squeezed her hand.

Nicole hopped, bouncing on her toes, good mood difficult to contain. Contentment seemed par for the course while holding her man-dragon's hand. She reveled in it, allowing happiness to seep in. A dangerous reaction. She'd learned often and early to mistrust happy, but here—right now—she didn't care. No one knew better than she did, life wasn't easy. It liked to throw curveballs. Made sure you paid attention and took nothing for granted, but with Vyroth, she'd roll with the punches.

Accept what came next.

And give him everything she had to offer.

Heavy footfalls echoing against stone, the guys

stopped at a dead end. Tempel murmured. The solid stone wall wavered then cleared, revealing a doorway. An acrid smell drifted over the threshold.

Vyroth jerked against her.

"Fuck," Cyprus growled.

"No!" With a roar, Tempel shot into the lair.

Ash kicked up in his wake. Grey flakes billowed into the tunnel.

The stomach-turning scent intensified, and Nicole realized what the awful smell meant—burnt flesh and dead dragons.

Letting go of her hand, Vyroth raced after Tempel.

Another heart-wrenching roar. The sound so pain-filled, so devastating her heart clenched and· her stomach pitched, throwing bile up her throat. "Cyprus."

"Stay here, Niki. We gotta lock him down before he loses—"

Heat blazed into the corridor.

Nicole crouched, getting low and, arms curved over her head, watched chunks of rock blasted through the magical doorway. The ground shuddered. The guys cursed. Solid stone cracked, opening fissures along the floor, fracturing the walls and ceiling.

The tunnel started to crumble as tremors turned into a violent earthquake.

Knocked backward, Rannock yelled at her.

Levin snarled.

Nicole moved.

"Nay, lass!" Reaching out, Cyprus tried to stop her.

Shooting past him, she leapt over debris in the doorway and raced into the lair. Heart thumping, feet moving, she took a quick snapshot. Broken fluorescent tubes hanging from the ceiling. Glass on the floor, a landing and damaged staircase slanting to her right.

Steel railing between her and a room full of furniture in front of her. Ash smeared across walls and piled in heaps on the floor.

Eyes aglow, magic surging, Tempel howled.

Ripped from the walls, huge rocks spun around him as he lost his mind in the center of the room. Shattered furniture and broken glass joined the magic-driven cyclone, levitating in air, getting sucked into whirling wreckage. Fighting to contain him, Vyroth shouted at Tempel, struggling to hang onto his friend in the midst of the tornado.

Planting her hand on the railing, Nicole vaulted over the railing. Her feet slammed down. Slipping on ash, focused on Tempel, she ducked beneath flying debris, fought the sidewinding slide, and propelled herself straight toward him.

Out of control, Tempel threw Vyroth aside.

Nicole took advantage of the opening and, running full tilt, slammed into him.

He hissed.

Locking her arms around him, she held on hard. Strong hands grabbed her shoulders. Fear lodged in her throat, she hung on as Tempel tried to pry her loose. His fingers raked across her back. Pain rippled. She ignored the burn, and clinging to him, used what she learned from Montgomery. Gritting her teeth, she reversed the process. Instead of shutting down the stream, she tapped into the Meridian, cranked the faucet wide open, and hammered him with energy.

The blast hit him like high voltage.

Jolting against her, Tempel stumbled backward.

The earthquake downgraded, moving from life threatening to intense rumble.

"Hold on to me, Tempel. Hold on, darlin'," she

said, using his endearment for her. "Hold on—hold on —hold on."

He made an indescribable sound. Agonizing. Soul-shattering. Heartbreaking.

"Dead," he rasped, his pain so stark tears filled her eyes. "They're dead... *dead*."

"I'm sorry." Hands fisted in the back of his coat, she hugged him harder. "So, so sorry, Tempel."

Quaking against her, he stopped pushing her away. His arms came around her. A quiet sob racked him. "Niki."

"Hold on, darlin'—just hold on."

Someone moved beside them.

Tears trailing down her cheeks, she reached for Vyroth.

His hand found hers. He laced their fingers together and, raising the other hand, cupped the back of Tempel's head. Holding her gaze, he watched her tears fall and spoke to his friend. Quiet voice. Soothing tones. Murmurs that amounted to nonsense while Tempel shook in her arms, and Vyroth wrapped his around them both, holding her and the warrior she consoled safe inside the strength of his embrace.

31

Heavy with grief, an unnatural silence hung in the air. The eerie stillness seeped through fissures torn in the wall by the earthquake, acting like a virus, poisoning everything it touched, infecting the Belarus lair with a sickness that would never be cured.

Shoulders planted against kitchen wall, surrounded by broken crockery and busted cabinetry, Vyroth watched his friend.

Tempel wasn't doing well.

To be expected after arriving home to find the warriors he called family dead. No. He frowned. Not just dead—betrayed, murdered, taken before their time by treachery.

He knew Tempel had a theory, but refused to ask. Or prompt him. Not yet. The male needed time. Time in the quiet. Time to acclimatize to his new reality. Time for grief to turn to rage and the burning desire to find the guilty one and end his life.

Vyroth understood how it worked.

He'd spent years doing the same, struggling to come to terms with the murders of his uncle and cousins. In truth, he wasn't done yet. Still didn't know what happened. Not exactly, but after talking with Cyprus he was closer to putting it together—to connecting the dots and finding the missing puzzle pieces.

Some of his questions answered.

The closure he'd sought for years. Maybe now, he could put the past behind him. Work with his brothers to move on and accept what he couldn't change. Finding Forge wouldn't right the wrong. Not that he'd ever stop looking. Forge was family. If his cousin really was alive, Vyroth needed to know. To make sure he was alright, understand why the male hadn't come home, and continued to stay away.

Dragging his mind from his pack's dark history, his gaze drifted back to his friend.

Expression blank, Tempel stood in front of the kitchen island. Muscles tensed. Body locked. Palms planted on the cracked countertop. Gaze fixed on the glass urns full of his comrades' ashes lined up in front of him.

Vyroth clenched his teeth. He couldn't bear it anymore. His friend's pain was agonizing to watch, difficult to swallow. He needed to *do something*—alleviate Tempel's suffering in some small way.

Pushing away from the wall, Vyroth crossed the kitchen. He stayed quiet, stepping over the shattered pendant lights on the floor, and headed for the high cabinet. With a flick, he opened one of the doors and pulled two tumblers from the top rack. Brackets torn from the wall, the cupboard listed sideways. Broken bowls and plates littered the first shelf. Shards of smashed pottery lay on the granite countertop.

He ignored the mess and, leaning sideways, yanked the freezer open. Hinges squawked. Scanning the interior, he reached inside. Ice went into the glasses, clinking against expensive crystal. Senses trained on Tempel, he grabbed an iced bottle by the neck.

Belarusian vodka.

Duck Wild Gold Filter.

Tested and true, VIP strong, a fan favorite.

Tumblers in hand, he reversed course and approached his friend. Setting the glasses on the countertop, Vyroth cranked the top off the bottle and poured. Chilled alcohol hit the ice. He didn't stop at one finger of alcohol. Being generous, he filled each glass three inches deep and put one of the tumblers in front of Tempel.

"Drink."

Without a word, Tempel shot the vodka, then held out the glass, asking for more.

Downing his portion, Vyroth tipped the bottle again. Duck Wild Gold sloshed against fine cut crystal, turning colorless liquid into a prism of color. He watched Tempel down the second dose and did the same.

Refill. Drink. Repeat.

Glass after glass.

He poured. They drank.

No words exchanged.

Two warriors standing shoulder-to-shoulder, in solidarity and silence. One male locked in grief so thick the other didn't know what to say.

Or how to help.

Turning his wrist, Tempel rattled the ice in his glass. "Where is everyone?"

"Looking around. Locking down the lair."

"Giving me time."

"Aye."

Tempel nodded. "Niki?"

"With Levin and Cyprus in the computer room."

"Anything working?"

He shook his head. "Smashed tae shite, brother."

"Traitor," Tempel murmured, staring into the bottom of his empty glass. "He betrayed us."

Talking at last. Sharing his thoughts.

Vyroth released a pent-up breath. "Achan. That who you mean?"

"Yeah."

"He's not here?" Shifting his stance, Vyroth turned and leaned his hip against the countertop. "Not among the fallen?"

"No." Brows furrowed, Tempel stared at the urns. "The asshole isn't here."

Vyroth poured more vodka. He stayed quiet and waited, drinking with his friend, employing patience, knowing Tempel needed to talk.

Raising his hands, Tempel gripped the back of his head. Fingers clenched his hair, he shook his head. "Fucking hell, man."

"Tell me."

"The lair is protected by an impenetrable spell. Keeps us hidden. Keeps us safe. Coded to our DNA. No one but the Belarus pack has access. He had to let them in. Must've..." Tempel's voice broke. Struggling to control his rage, he flexed his hands in his hair, then let go and raised his head. Green-rimmed eyes full of pain struck him. "My pack is strong. So strong, Vyroth. Warriors all. No way the enemy found our lair—or got inside. Not without help."

"Two for one." Vyroth murmured, spinning his tumbler in a circle. Vodka sloshed as glass rasped against granite and an idea took root. "A second mission tae lay at Levin's feet."

Tempel frowned. "What?"

"Lev's good, Tempel," he said, laying out the plan, the best way forward. "The absolute best. You need information and a male found. Lev'll unearth the intel. So aye—two birds, one stone. He's already on Montgomery's trail. We'll put him on your pack too—find the bastards responsible. Give us a target to hunt and kill."

A muscle twitched in Tempel's jaw. "I'm not going with you, Vyroth. I'm staying here."

"Think again, lad. You're not staying here," he said, tone firm, digging in, knowing he had one shot to convince his friend. Tempel wanted to disappear. Planned to bury himself beneath the pain, hunt alone and exact his revenge. A terrible plan, and he should know. He'd spent years alone, out wandering the world, trying to make sense of his own pain. "You've already lost one pack today. You'll not be losing another."

"But... I'm not Scottish."

"So? Families arenae built by country alone." Tipping his head back, Vyroth downed the rest of his drink. "You're my brother—word, deed, attitude. Proved it time and again in prison. Havenae wavered since. You're coming tae the Highlands, Tempel. Best work on the brogue."

Surprise in his eyes, Tempel opened his mouth, no doubt to say something stupid.

"Shut it," he said as his younger brother walked into the kitchen.

Laptop in hand, Tydrin tipped his chin. "All settled?"

"Aye. Official. Tempel's joining us in Aberdeen."

Purple gaze fixed on the jars, Tydrin nodded. "Good."

Palming Tempel's shoulder, Vyroth squeezed, then

pointed to the computer his brother held. "Whatcha got, Ty?"

"Found one they didn't smash." Picking up a downed stool, Tydrin set it on its feet and sat down. Wiping dust off the countertop, he set the computer on the clean patch. "Need the flash drive."

Digging into his front pocket, Vyroth fished the memory stick out of his jeans and handed to him. "It's encrypted."

"I know," his brother said. "I'm going tae e-mail it tae Ivy."

Vyroth blinked. *E-mail.* Seriously? "Since when do you know how to use a computer?"

"Since I met and mated a hacker."

A what? His brows popped skyward.

"Top five in the world, V." Looking proud, fingers flying over laptop keys, Tydrin's mouth curved. "My female—wicked smart. She can hack into anything."

A *swoosh* echoed through the kitchen.

Silence followed.

Seconds ticked past, turning into minutes, feeding the stillness. The hush spiraled out from the island, drifting across the great room where he'd conjured the urns and helped Tempel gather the ashes.

Back to being quiet, Tempel reached out and touched the top of the urns. Grief fogging the air around him, he bowed his head. Vyroth's chest went tight. Fuck. It wasn't fair. Wasn't right. Couldn't be understood. Expected or not, death of a loved one never made sense... and wasn't easy to accept.

Tempel took his hands from what remained of his pack.

Tydrin shifted on the stool. "You want tae bury them here, Tempel? Is there a special place? A spot—"

Tempel growled. "They come with me."

"Whatever you need, brother," Tydrin said, voice full of compassion.

Leaning sideways, Vyroth bumped shoulders with his friend. Tempel dipped his chin, acknowledging the show of support and—

Strong current sparked over Vyroth's skin.

As the charge intensified, tense muscles relaxed.

Vyroth exhaled in relief. Nicole. She was walking his way, keeping pace as his packmates searched the Belarus lair. The steady tap of footfalls echoed. The rambling beat spread across the great room as his brothers descended the staircase.

Cyprus in the lead.

Nicole behind him.

Levin and Rannock bringing up the rear.

Skirting broken furniture, Cyprus strode into the kitchen. As he joined the cluster around the island, he looked at Tydrin. "Sent?"

"Aye. She's waiting for the file. The second she—"

The computer pinged.

"That was fast. Let's see what she unlocked." Using the track pad, his brother scrolled down. "Shite."

"What?" he asked, reaching for Nicole. Rounding the end of the island, she slipped beneath his arm. Kissing the top of her head, he tucked her against his side, but kept his gaze on his brother. "Good or bad?"

Eyes glued to the screen, Tydrin shrugged. "Video files. A bunch of 'em."

One hand planted on the countertop, Cyprus leaned toward the computer, getting a better look. "Open one."

"Donnae know what's in it, Cy." Hesitating, fingers hovering over the trackpad, Tydrin glanced at Nicole, then at him.

Quick to understand, she gave him a squeeze. "Need a bathroom break. I'll be back."

"Thanks, *Tazleiah*," he murmured, watching her go. "Donnae go far."

Meeting his gaze over her shoulder, she rolled her eyes.

He grinned, then moved around the island, joining his packmates on the other side.

Lowering the volume, waiting until Nicole was out of range, Tydrin double-clicked on the first file. A video started to play. Blurry shot. Water pebbled on the camera lens. Damp stone wall in the background. Seconds ticked past. Someone wiped the droplets away, then swung the camera around and—

Vyroth sucked in a sharp breath.

"Bloody hell," Cyprus said, surprise on his face.

Shock faded as revulsion and outrage spiked, rolling off his brothers-in-arms.

The urge to hurl the computer across the kitchen took hold. Locking it down, Vyroth shut off his disgust and forced himself to watch. To pay attention. Notice the details. Collect information in the hopes it might prove useful later on.

He focused on the warrior.

A big male strapped to an electrified vertical grill. Arms and legs spread wide and handcuffed to the steel bars. One eye swollen shut, the other one blazing with fury, burns and cuts crisscrossed his bare torso. His torturer standing off to the side, beside a table laid with lethal-looking tools, threatening the warrior with more extreme pain.

Something about pulling his canines.

The male grinned, taunting the bastard, daring him to do it.

Vyroth twitched as recognition thumped through

him. Hellfire. He knew the warrior. Had seen him somewhere before. On one of his trips. While in...

He curled his hand into a fist. "Cyprus."

His twin snarled in reply.

"I recognize him."

Tydrin hit pause.

Everyone exhaled in relief.

Cyprus raised a brow. "Which one?"

"The male strapped to the grill," he said, digging for the memory, trying place the warrior. He ran through his activities in Prague when searching for information about Forge. The festival. The restaurants and bars. The Emblem Club, a cigar lounge owned by a member of the Archguard. "Gage. His name is Gage. He's a Nightfury."

"Bastian's pack." Shoving Tydrin's hand out of the way, Levin tapped the play button. "Who's the sadist torturing him?"

As the question left Levin's mouth, the bastard turned toward the camera holding a pair of plyers.

"Zidane," Tempel said, voice full of fury. "Rodin's firstborn. Commander of the Russian pack."

Rannock threw him an incredulous look. "Highborn. Dragonkind elite. Pretty bold tae put this shite on camera."

Vyroth stared at his friend. "You sure?"

"One hundred percent." Tempel's upper lip curled. "We've been feuding with the Russian pack for years. I'd know the asshole anywhere."

"Turn it off. I've seen enough," Cyprus said, stepping back, putting distance between him and the video. "How many more are there?"

Tydrin snapped the laptop closed. "Dozens."

Rannock scowled. "Totally fucked up."

"But useful," Vyroth murmured, wanting to kiss

Lapier for risking his life to get him the information. "Ty—does Ivy have hooks in the dark web."

"Aye."

"Send another e-mail. We need her to find a way to reach Bastian."

Levin's mouth curved in approval.

Tydrin cracked the computer back open.

"Heard rumblings in Prague." Watching his brother type, Vyroth examined what he'd learned while gathering intel. Pieces of the Archguard jigsaw puzzle snapped together. The disquiet at the festival. The division between attending packs. Rodin's reported hatred of Bastian. "The Nightfuries are moving against Rodin and the Archguard. They want a new order. Equal power across the board. Every Dragonkind pack gets a seat at the table."

"Roundtable tactics." Arms crossed over his chest, Rannock rocked back on his heels. "Stuff of legends."

"Well, then, no time tae lose. A discussion with the Nightfury commander is definitely in order," Cyprus said, a nasty gleam in his eyes. "Pack it up, lads. V— collect yer mate. Time tae head home."

Home.

Sounded good to him.

After months of being away, he longed for the Cairngorms and the smell of Highland heather. But as Vyroth turned into a corridor, following the buzz in his veins, looking for his mate, unease sparked. So much information to gather. So many problems to solve. Lots of room for error. Little time to accomplish his goals, if what he suspected about the Nightfury pack held true and Bastian made his move before Vyroth was ready.

32

Skimming the treetops, Warsaw on his wing, Montgomery flew over the old hunting lodge. Sloping metal roof. Stone-stacked chimneys pumping out twin streams of smoke. The smell of juniper in the air. No one in the backyard.

He circled back around, making a wider sweep of the area.

Nothing but forest for miles. No humans living anywhere near the newly commissioned wildlife reserve, but... a male could never be too careful. And given the message—more like summons—he'd received at dusk, he refused to take any chances.

Or risk a run-in with Rodin.

The leader of the Archguard wouldn't appreciate a visit from him. At any time, but certainly not at his private hunting cabin outside of Prague.

Focused on the structure nestled between old-growth trees, he fine-tuned his sonar. Magic rolled out in front of him as he scanned the interior. His eyes narrowed. Three males inside the lodge. None stationed around the perimeter.

Montgomery released a slow breath. Poisonous mist escaped on his exhale, pissing him off. Nervous energy always messed with his dragon half, making it difficult for him to control the venom in his veins.

Which pissed him off even more.

He shouldn't be tense. Shouldn't be worried about the meeting, but... old habits died hard. He couldn't relax. Recent events had strung him tight, and no wonder. After being cornered by Vyroth and watching his castle burn, taking anything for granted equated to a bad idea. The message sounded cordial enough, but he needed to be ready... for anything—whatever curveball his older brother planned to throw at him.

Making one more pass, he spiraled into an updraft, then folded his wings. Gravity grabbed hold. Night vision sharp, he dropped between a break in the trees. His paws touched down on the driveway. Pine needles jumped. Gravel in the circular drive scattered, tumbling into the low wall of the long-neglected fountain as Warsaw landed behind him.

The outside light came on, blinding him for a second.

Turning his head, he allowed his eyes to adjust, then scanned the wide porch.

Standing on the top step, shoulder propped against an ancient post, his older brother watched him prowl around the defunct Koi pond. "Shift, Monty."

The low growl settled his scales. Deep baritone wrapped in a Russian accent. Familiar. Safe. A steadying sound, the immovable force of the male who'd spent a lifetime protecting him from their sire—sending him to boarding school in America, shepherding him through his *first shift*, teaching him how to fight, raising him as his own.

Meeting his brother's pitch-black gaze, he transformed and conjured his clothes. He strode forward.

His brother met him at the bottom of the stairs and pulled him into a fierce hug.

"It's been too long, little brother."

"Fuck, Zidane," he muttered, embracing him back. "It's good to see you. Missed you."

"Then why'd you stay away so long?"

"You know why."

"Father's softened his stance."

Montgomery scoffed. "From what? Hatred to indifference?"

"Well," Zidane said, hedging. "At least, he's no longer trying to kill you."

"Actively, anyway."

"Progress, Monty. A little goes a long way."

Right.

Zidane had the luxury of believing the maxim. Their sire loved him. Celebrated the day he'd been born. Showered him with affection. Trusted him to carry out Archguard-sanctioned missions.

Hooking an arm around his neck, Zidane drew him toward the lodge. "Glad you came, Monty."

"What do you need?" Accustomed to doing favors for Zidane, he walked up the stairs. Wide planks creaked as he crossed the veranda toward the front door. Yakapov, his brother's first-in-command—stood in the doorway. He tipped his chin in greeting. The blond giant returned the gesture, then retreated inside, leaving the door open behind him. "Got a job for me?"

He could use one.

After the mess in Black Forest, he needed a quick cash infusion. Down and dirty. Quick and clean. He didn't care what kind of mission. The contracts Zidane kicked his way always paid well. A couple of months spent solving Archguard problems behind the scenes would offset his recent losses. Recharge his bank account and put him back in the hunt.

"Come inside." Tilting his head, Zidane motioned to the door. "I'll explain."

Intrigued, Montgomery followed his brother over the threshold. He swept the area. His mouth curved. Same cabin, same old interior. Nothing new. Comfortable leather couches, deep-cushioned armchairs arranged around the massive stone fireplace. The smell of cigar smoke. The sight of a well-laid grill. Yakapov settled in his usual spot—in a leather chair pulled close to hearth, booted feet crossed at the ankles, legs stretched toward the fire.

His focus drifted toward the open-plan kitchen. Pine cabinetry yellowed by time and... a warrior he'd never seen before sitting on the island, shoveling a spoonful of puddling into his mouth.

Zidane gestured to the unknown male. "Monty, meet Achan. Newest member of my death squad."

Montgomery raised a brow. "Death squad?"

"Sanctioned. Papers signed, sealed, and delivered."

"Official channels? Not rubber-stamped behind closed doors?"

"Archguard approved. Completely aboveboard." A satisfied gleam in his eyes, Zidane smiled. "I'm jumping the pond, Monty. Crossing the Atlantic to hunt Bastian and the Nightfuries."

The news hit him like a lightning strike. "Holy shit."

Tickled by his amazement, Zidane chuckled. "*Xzinile*, brother. It's open season on the asshole."

Good news for his brother.

Better news for their sire.

Rodin hated Bastian. Had tried to kill him for years—financing Ivar and the Razorback pack's feud with the Nightfury pack. Only to achieve abysmal results.

"I want you with me, little brother. Could use your skills. You hunt like no other warrior I know," Zidane said, throwing out compliments, turning the screws, hoping to convince him.

Stopping in front of a side table, his brother picked up a bottle of vodka, popped the top, and poured. Clear liquid hit the bottom of two glasses, sending the smell of alcohol across the lodge. Tumblers cupped in one hand, Zidane turned. His gaze flicked over Montgomery's best friend.

Tension flickered through him. Gaze sharp on his brother, Montgomery rolled his shoulders. "If I agree, it's a package deal. Warsaw comes with me."

Handing him a glass, Zidane shrugged. "You trust him, then I trust him."

He stared at his brother, an idea sharpening inside his mind. A safe haven for Warsaw. Cover for him inside a sanctioned death squad. Protection from Rodin after losing control of both Vyroth and Tempel.

Lots of upside.

A tempting scenario.

Turning the glass in his hand, Montgomery examined the pros and cons of his brother's proposal anyway. Lined up the angles. Identified possible pitfalls. Studied the scheme from all sides and... hell. He couldn't discount the advantages.

Zidane offered a perfect solution to his problem. He needed out of Europe for a while. Staying off the Scottish pack's radar until he decided how to deal with them sounded like a good idea. Avoiding his less-than-loving sire included a number of health benefits as well.

Time away—to think and regroup.

Time spent half a world away with his older brother.

He glanced at Warsaw, asking his opinion without words.

Arms crossed, stance wide, standing just inside the door, his friend nodded.

Montgomery turned back to his brother. "We're in."

Satisfaction alive in his dark eyes, Zidane tipped his glass. Montgomery raised his own, clinked the rim against his brother's, then downed the shot, excited about the turn of events... and his imminent trip to America.

33

ABERDEEN, SCOTLAND – THREE WEEKS LATER

Thunder rumbled in the distance. Driving rain struck the floor-to-ceiling windows in her new workshop. Droplets streaked across the glass as Nicole plugged in her Canon EOS Rebel and uploaded the before and after pictures. As images transferred from camera to computer, she glanced at the antique clock hanging next to the industrial vent hood. She calculated the time difference, then sat in her ergonomic rolling chair and leaned toward the Pro Retina display screen.

New technology.

State of the art.

The best money could buy.

Completely ridiculous. Her man-dragon was out of control.

She was a salvage hunter, selling fixed up, super-fly vintage stuff in an on-line store. Not the CEO of a public corporation pulling down millions a year. Nor did she want to be. She loved her little store of old treasures. Liked interacting with buyers from a distance, not up close and personal. Enjoyed printing off shipping labels from her dented printer with peeling plastic. She didn't need a new laser *whatever-the-hell* Ivy called it.

Too bad Vyroth couldn't help himself.

He wanted the best for her. Nothing but the latest new-fangled thing would do.

Hunting for an icon on the wide screen, Nicole slid her finger over the trackpad, then sighed. She wasn't upset with Vyroth. Not really. She understood what drove him and, in all honesty, should leave him be— let him do what he needed to in his quest to take care of her. The way he treated her—how seriously he took her work, her passion for refurbishing things most considered junk—was testament to her importance to him. He showed her every day how much he loved her.

And she appreciated it.

Really, she did. Enjoyed watching how much he got out of spoiling her, but...

Seriously.

The shopping sprees needed to stop.

If one more high-tech gadget showed up in her vintage-inspired, low-tech world, she'd lose her ever-loving mind.

"Ah," she murmured, finding the icon.

Positioning the cursor, she clicked. A video chat box opened in the middle of the monitor. Cinderblock came into view. Vertical toolboxes, painted fire engine red, stood like soldiers against the unpainted wall, a tattered American flag tacked above the neat row. Her gaze strayed to the stack of dog-eared papers and assorted tools strewn across a steel-topped mechanic bench. Dressed in coveralls, her sister collapsed into the ratty chair sitting in front of her make-shift desk at the back of the garage.

Nicole smiled, waving her arms around. "Hey!"

A grease smudge on her cheek, welding goggles perched on her head, Cate snorted. "You're a dork."

"Yeah, okay... whatever," she said, still grinning.

Setting an electric drill on the table, Cate picked up her cellphone. The picture tilted, then righted again. "Get the packages I sent?"

"The boxes arrived yesterday. Thanks for sending my gear."

"A girl can't be without her tools. What would become of the world?"

"Catastrophe."

"Without a doubt," Cate said, a sparkle in her eyes. Blonde and blue-eyed, her sister looked a lot like her, but in reverse—light to her dark. The Yin to her Yang. "Where's your man?"

Nicole tapped into the hum, tracking Vyroth's proximity to her workshop. "On his way."

"What'd he buy you today?"

"Nothing, God willing."

Cate laughed.

"When you coming?"

"Two weeks. I booked my flight today."

"Yay!" she screeched, chair dancing, waving her arms around again.

"Seriously. You need to stop doing that, Niki—total dorksville."

She ignored the advice. Cate was the epitome of cool, not her. "You gonna be able to finish the '67 Chevy on time?"

"The Corvette isn't the problem. I'm on track to finish the restoration with a couple of days to spare," Cate said, blowing out a breath. "Dad's the issue."

"MIA again?"

"Two days... no word. He's not answering his cell."

"Crap." Their freaking father. The personification

of bad ideas, too restless to stay put, he often disappeared. A day here, a couple of days there. It didn't happen a lot anymore, but when it happened, she and her sister worried. Nothing good ever followed when he jumped the fence. "Terry?"

Cate sighed. "Pissed off. I would be too."

"The man's a saint."

"Don't know how he does it, Niki. I'da been long gone by now."

Wasn't that the truth.

A strong woman, her sister knew her own mind and didn't take crap from anyone. Dad included. When home, Nicole played the role of troubleshooter, acting as the go-between, keeping things even-keeled between the two. But her ability to intervene was now a thing of the past. As much she hated to leave Cate, she wasn't going home.

She'd made her decision.

No going back.

She needed to stick to the plan, concentrate on building a new life with Vyroth and the Scottish pack, but... man, it was hard. Hard to watch her sister struggle. Hard to be so far away. Hard to leave Cate to deal with the mess that was their father on her own.

"No guilt, sis," Cate said, reading her expression. "You got a good thing going over there. Hang onto it and that man of yours."

Her throat went tight. "Love my baby sister."

"She loves you back." Rounding the front bumper of a car, Cate winked at her. "Now, I gotta go. If I'm getting on a plane in two weeks, I need to finish this bitch."

"Tomorrow?"

"Same time, same number."

Nicole nodded.

The picture cut out as Cate ended the call.

"Two weeks," Vyroth said from behind her. "The lads are going to lose their minds when she rolls into the lair."

Swiveling in her fancy-ass office chair, Nicole smiled at her man-dragon. "I've already warned Rannock I'll shoot him if he touches her."

"Her choice, *Tazleiah*." Mischief in his eyes, Vyroth pushed away from his lean against the door frame. "Lots of pleasure on offer here if she wants it."

She fake-frowned at him. "Only if there isn't any dragon brainwashing involved."

Vyroth chuckled, then put himself in gear, rounding the huge work surface in the center of her workshop. Unable to lay eyes on him without wanting to touch, Nicole met him halfway. Not slowing, she bumped into, then settled against him. Her arms went around his neck. His hands slid into the back pockets of her jeans.

She tipped her face up, asking for a kiss.

He gave her what she wanted. Dipping his head, he tangled his tongue with hers, delivering his taste, making her want more. Deep kisses turned into softer ones. Big hands moved into sweeping caresses. Cupping her ass, he lifted her off her feet. Addicted to the feel of him, Nicole wrapped her legs around his hips, encouraging him as he set her down on the worktable, next to a beat-up typewriter.

Snug between her thighs, he nipped her bottom lip.

"Yum," she whispered against his mouth. Fingers playing in his thick hair, she kissed him again, taking the lead, needing him again. Which was... crazy. She'd already had him today. After she'd woken wrapped around him in bed, before Cyprus called him away. "How was the meeting?"

He growled. "Frustrating."

"Still nothing?"

"Lapier's filled in a lot of the blanks, but Montgomery..." His hands flexed on her waist. "He's smoke. No sign of the bastard, and Levin's been looking —hard."

Trying to soothe him, she stroked the nape of his neck. "You'll find him, Vyroth. He'll make a mistake. Pop his head up, and you'll—"

"Rip it off."

"Well," she said, amusement curling through her. "I was going to say *get him*, but ripping his head off works too."

He grunted. "Nothing from the Nightfury pack either."

"Give Ivy time. She'll figure out how to reach them."

Caressing her back, Vyroth leaned in to kiss her throat. Neatly trimmed instead of ragged, his beard brushed her skin. Pleasure shivered through her. She kissed the shell of his ear. He purred and pressed his advantage, slipping his hands beneath the hem of her shirt.

Warm, calloused palms against her skin.

Heat gathered in her veins.

She rolled her hips against him.

He licked over her pulse point. "How about I give you some of my time instead?"

Tipped her head back, she arched into his next caress. "Now?"

"Right here, right now."

"The door."

Mouth brushing her collarbone, he murmured a

command. Hinges creaked as the door swung closed. She heard the lock turn and raised her arms. Slow, sure, driving her crazy, Vyroth drew the shirt over her head, then went after her jeans. The work of seconds he stripped her, laying her bare on the tabletop.

His fingers found her. Stroked. Played. Made her writhe as he set himself at her entrance and—

"Oh, man... crazy good." She moaned as he thrust inside her.

So hard. So deep. Moving fast. Hammering her with pleasure.

"Hands," he growled against her breast.

Doing what he taught her—what he liked, what drove him wild—she crossed her hands and stretched her arms over her head.

One hand wrapped around her stacked wrists, he held her down and powered in. "Hold on, Niki. Gonna ride you hard."

Perfect. Beautiful. The absolute best.

"No mercy, Vyroth."

"None."

"Love you, honey," she whispered, same as always. Every time she held him. Every time he moved inside her. "Love you."

"Love you too, Niki."

"Forever."

"And always." He groaned as she arched, rolling her hips, meeting him stroke for stroke. "Fuck. Beautiful. Dream come true, baby. All I'll ever need. All I'll ever want... my dream girl."

His dream girl.

She loved that he thought so.

Reveled in the idea he believed she was made and meant for him.

Closing her eyes, Nicole listened to the rain fall

against the windows and rode with him, memorizing the feel, connected to the source, absorbing his love for her. Intense need. Honest connection. Glorious oblivion. Just the way she needed it to be, and... he was right. All she'd ever need. All she'd ever want. Vyroth was perfect for her in every way.

Gratefulness whispered through her.

Lucky.

She was so lucky to have found him. Fortunate the universe intervened to show her the way. Leading her to Vyroth. Placing him in her path. Giving her what she hadn't known she wanted, but now knew she couldn't live without—a happy ending, the promise of a beautiful future, with the man-dragon in her arms.

A NOTE FROM THE AUTHOR

Thank you for taking the time to read *Fury of Persuasion*. If you enjoyed it, please help others find my books so they can enjoy them too.

Recommend it: Please help other readers find this book by recommending it to friends, readers' groups, and discussion boards.

Review it: Let other readers know what you liked or didn't like about *Fury of Persuasion*.

Lend it: This e-book is lending-enabled, so feel free to share it with your friends. Sign up for my newsletter to receive new release information and other freebies. You can follow me on Facebook or on Twitter under @coreenecallahan.

Book updates can be found at www.CoreeneCallahan.com

Thanks again for taking the time to read my books!

ALSO BY COREENE CALLAHAN

Dragonfury Scotland

Fury of a Highland Dragon

Fury of Shadows

Fury of Denial

Fury of Persuasion

Dragonfury Short Story Collection

Fury of Fate

Fury of Conviction

Dragonfury Series

Fury of Fire

Fury of Ice

Fury of Seduction

Fury of Desire

Fury of Obsession

Fury of Surrender

Fury of Destruction

Circle of Seven Series

Knight Awakened

Knight Avenged

Warriors of the Realm Series

Warrior's Revenge